# No words

# *No Words*

*Reneé Kimberling*

Milo House Press

Copyright © 2003, No Words, Reneé Kimberling, All rights reserved.

ISBN: 1-59268-044-5

Milo House Press

GMAPublishing.com
Check out our website
GMA is a global publishing company
Our books are available and distributed around the world and can be found on the internet at Amazon, Barnes and Noble and any major bookseller.

GMAPublishing@aol.com

All rights reserved. No portion of this book may be reproduced, stored in a retrieval system, or transmitted in any form or by any other means- electronic, mechanical, photocopy, recording or any other except for brief quotations in printed reviews, without the prior permission of the publisher.

Cover Layout: Christina Gubbins
Senior Portraits on Cover: Gary St. Martin
Family Portrait on Cover: Olan Mills Studio
Manuscript Assistant: John Beanblossom

Printed in the United States of America

*To my children, Kelly and Ron -*

*I cherish each day of your lives.*

*In memory and honor of Jill and Jeff Rosko -*

*You'll remain in our hearts forever.*

# *Author's Note*

*This is a true story, without exaggerations or distortions of events. It is a story of love, utterly tragic loss, and ultimate survival as told by the two people who lived it – Janet and Tom Rosko. We owe Janet and Tom our utmost appreciation for their willingness to share their lives and their tragedies in such an open and uncensored manner. It is my sincere hope that in the end it will prove a catharsis to them as well as the many people who have shared their losses. However, I fully realize I have asked them over the course of many months to relive, and in fact dissect, the darkest periods of their lives. It has not been an easy journey for them.*

*Their story is told through two different perspectives – that of Janet's and also of Tom's. This gives us a broader view of the entire story yet also allows us to experience the memories and emotions that are unique to each of them. Selected chapters are related in a conversational tone, giving the reader insight into their camaraderie, devotion, and mutual concerns.*

*Tom and Janet were always worried they would not have enough to say. On the contrary, I think they have quite a lot to say and much to teach the rest of us.*

# 1

# Janet

Once you've seen one Rosko, you've seen them all. Tom had three brothers, and when you saw any one of them, you just knew he was a Rosko. In fact, even his mother has a hard time now looking through the old pictures, trying to remember which one is which.

My brother Chuck actually knew Tom before I did, at least knew *of* him. We were all students at Tolleston High in Gary, Indiana, but at that time Tom wasn't too interested in knowing my brother; what he really wanted was to know me.

In the spring of 1962, Tom was nearing the end of his senior year, and I was a junior. He was a good-looker all right, with thick dark hair and gorgeous big brown eyes, not too tall but tall enough. One of the girls I hung out with thought he was a real heart-throb and had quite a crush on him, though when I looked at him, I never thought, "Wow!" I just knew him as a nice guy who came from a nice family, and when I was around him I felt very comfortable and secure. Some may think that sounds boring, but in high school I was backward and quiet, so for me that's saying a lot. He was a gentleman.

I had a car in school – one of the lucky girls who did. Every morning I drove my dad to work and then picked up my girlfriends. We would hang out in the school parking lot for a while before class and sure enough Tom and his buddies gradually worked their way closer and closer. Eventually they started talking to us, and then the day came when Tom mustered the nerve to ask me out.

I have friends who can recall every detail of their first date forty-five years ago – down to what they wore – but I don't even remember where Tom and I went. I'm pretty sure we just went to the Blaze Drive-In, which back then was the local high school hang-out. It's not like I had so many dates before Tom that our first date would get lost in a haze of romantic escapades. In fact there weren't *any* notable dates before him! I guess the only important thing is that once I started going out with Tom I never dated any other guy. Maybe we were just meant to be.

You see, there wasn't anything I didn't like about him. He wasn't perfect – nobody is, but there was nothing about him that made me think, "Okay Janet, what are you doing here with him?" We just fit, like a strand of pearls with a basic black dress or a hot, sunny day for a Fourth of July picnic. We fit, we blended. His sense of humor tickled me in all the right places, and if I ever needed someone, I was comfortable he would be there. He was my rock.

For me, that security was important. I wasn't the normal, adventurous teenage girl - flirty and perhaps even a little reckless. I was the one who went tobogganing just to fit in with the group but never even made it down the hill! I wouldn't even go horseback riding! I was afraid of everything. Not Tom, though. In fact, he was a bit of a show-off and that took me a while to get used to. He had been the baby in his family for eight years before his mother was suddenly shocked by the fourth boy, and personally I think he spent his teenage years vying for attention, or maybe it was the "Napoleon complex," where as a smaller guy he just felt he had to be mighty to offset his build. Whatever it was, he would rev his engine, spin his tires, and generally draw attention to himself. But most times we just hung out with our gang at the Blaze.

Come to think of it, I did go out with someone after I started dating Tom. I had already made a commitment to go to my Senior Prom with a fellow named Jerry. Guys had always seemed to overlook me and when Jerry asked me to Prom, I thought, "You know what? Wow! Somebody asked me out!" So I said, "Yes! Of course! Sure!" I had never gone to a Prom before. And then he turned out to be class president too! How many girls would turn that down? Although Tom and I weren't real serious yet, he didn't like the idea. I did feel guilty, but...

# 2

# Tom

After our first date I began thinking that a guy just couldn't do any better than Janet. I don't know what made me pick her out of the crowd, but I started noticing her late in my senior year of high school. She was nice enough to look at with a small, friendly face that tilted down and to the side every time she smiled. She had brown hair and a knock-out shape. Definitely the quiet type, she wasn't at all like the other girls – like her friend Diane, for instance. Diane was more outgoing, and you could tell that right away. Janet was shy and took more of a back seat to things.

I kept right on noticing her, and finally, I just decided it was going to happen. Even though I didn't really know her, I wanted to, so I started talking to her and ended up asking her out.

I took her to the Blaze Drive-In in this '51 Plymouth Coupe that my dad had bought. It was only a two-seater but it had this big back end that could fit a bench for an extra person. He bought it from an older man that drove it back and forth to church on Sundays – really! I think it only had about 1500 miles on it when we got it. It was a little six-cylinder stick shift and I drove it to school, out with the guys, and of course to take Janet to the root beer stand for the first time.

Well, we hung out for a while and then I took her home. Although I can't say specifically what I liked about her, I knew we'd be going out again. We just seemed to get along. I liked being with her, and we never did get bored with each other.

We more or less started going steady, I guess you'd call it. Once in a while we'd go to the drive-in theater or just buzz around in the coupe, and occasionally I went over to her house. Her parents seemed to like me well enough, or perhaps you could say her mother liked me, but she didn't like me, you know? I didn't understand why, but probably because I was a boy and a Catholic one at that. Her dad was real nice, though. I never had a problem with him. Her brother had gone to our high school, but I wasn't too familiar with him because he was older. Her younger sister Betty, however, always liked me and many times she ended up tagging along on our dates. We'd set up a bench in the back of the coupe and she got a kick out of sitting there, so we just let her ride along.

I was under the impression that once we started dating, we would be exclusive. I already knew that I wasn't interested in going out with anybody else, and I thought Janet felt the same. Then she informed me she "already committed" herself to going to her Senior Prom with this other guy! Luckily for her, I ended up getting sick so I couldn't have taken her anyway. Don't know how I would have felt about that otherwise.

Nevertheless, our relationship went from one date to two, to weeks, to months. There were a couple of times when Janet thought maybe we should start seeing other people. I didn't want to and of course I didn't want her dating anyone else, but that never came about anyway because an hour later, she'd change her mind. We just got along good together, we did things together, and we grew on each other. We hit it off. I never had the feeling that this was meant to be or anything like that. I simply felt she was what I wanted and I had made up my mind. I can't even say I was the type of person who really knew his own mind – especially at that age – but I did as far as she was concerned. Obviously, I knew how to pick a good woman.

# 3

# Janet

My family lived in a modest little house on 10<sup>th</sup> and Bigger in Gary. We didn't have much when I was growing up, but there was a lot of love.

I'm the middle child of three. My brother Chuck is four years older and my sister Betty is two years younger. My father didn't work in the steel mill like most men in our area; he worked as a salesman at a tire store. Our last name was Coppess - my dad was Charlie and mom was Helen.

My dad was a simple person, a very good person. He didn't have anything bad to say about anybody. He was quiet, gentle, and dedicated to his family. He worked six days a week and had no outside interests – just came home to all of us. We were his world and there was nothing he wouldn't do for us, and our contentment came from just being together. Once in a while Mom would take us to Miller Beach, and then Dad would come join us after work for a cook-out, or we visited my Aunt Bertha, who lived close by. Sometimes we would just take a drive to a local farm to buy milk and eggs. It was a simple life.

My mom was a good mom. She stayed home and took care of us, the way most mothers did back then. She was there to get us ready for school and our breakfasts were always on the table. She was there when we came home. At six o'clock every night she served dinner and the five of us always ate together, and on Saturdays we ate an hour earlier. On Sundays we had a big breakfast and then spent the day together. Her family was her only focus.

Mom made sure my brother and sister and I followed her rules. She was a very stern woman. Her father was stern too, the kind that would say, "When you live under this roof, you live by these rules." I think my mother picked up a lot of that. My dad was laid back and would just say, "Come on now, kids." Mom was the one who ruled.

I was quiet and timid and pretty much stayed home all the time. I was afraid of everything. I was afraid of the dark, afraid of this or that. I don't know why. I also had a lot of inferiority complexes to roll over, though I don't know what I had to feel inferior about. I just lacked self-confidence. I used to make my sister go places with me – she boosted my bravery!

There was nothing really bad I could have gotten into anyway. Back in the early '50s things were uncomplicated. We played kick the can in the street. There was a big sand pile in the alleyway behind our house, and we used to make a fire on top of the sand and have a potato bake. Just a simple life. I don't think we even had a TV for a long, long time.

Only my mom and her sister Bertha lived in the area. If we had Thanksgiving by our house, Aunt Bertha had Christmas. One or the other, there was never any question about where we were going. Christmas was a special event – my mom went big at Christmas time. All the things we couldn't afford during the year she made up for at Christmas. Our Christmas tree was always huge and we had a small house! If you ever talked to my friends they'd tell you we consistently had the ugliest tree. It was either crooked or had bare spots – we just weren't very good judges of Christmas trees! But they were pretty to us. I just knew we had a good, steadfast family. Some people needed money to be happy, but we had love and security.

My mother taught us to play pinochle. We played just about anything to keep ourselves occupied - rummy too. She taught all the kids in the neighborhood in fact, and we weren't allowed to cheat. Once she caught you cheating you were out of the game and you weren't permitted to play anymore. I think that stemmed from her father. Mom claimed she had seen where her dad, if somebody would cheat at cards, would take the deck and throw it in the pot-bellied stove and that was that. You just didn't cheat. It was very simple. He solved the problem right away -

very straightforward. By God that was his house, and you did what he said.

I had a good friend then that I still have now. Her name is Diane and she lived close by down the alley. We're the same age – only a month between us. We started being friends in grade school, probably around 1951. We would be close for a while and then apart for a while, when she would hang around with some older girls, but then we always got back together. Once we hit junior high we were constantly a pair, and then she spent about ninety percent of her time at my house. She was crazy about my dad. Everyone liked my dad, he was so easy-going and he always wanted to go the extra mile for people. Anyway, if Diane was over and it was getting dark, I would sit in the alley and watch her go home, or we would walk to the middle of the street (it would have to be the exact mid-way point) then we would each go back our own way. I don't know why we've remained this close for this long, maybe opposites really do attract.

I worked at Art's Bakery through high school. I saved the money or bought school clothes for my sister and me. Like I said, my father didn't have a lot of money. It just wasn't there with three kids.

It sounds strange hearing me reminisce about all those years with my family. It seems like such a long time ago, and things were so very much simpler then.

# 4

# Tom

Growing up in the Rosko family was pretty unremarkable. We were the typical middle-income suburban Catholic family. Just average - nothing extraordinary - but then again I imagine most families would describe themselves as being average, until that one thing happens that changes their lives forever.

My dad was a ladle craneman in the #2 open-hearth furnace at Inland Steel Company. When you work on the ladle crane you're over all the heat – you're pouring the hot steel into ingots and the heat rises. Many times my dad's hands were so badly burned from the controls that he came home with them wrapped in rags. Finally, about five years short of retirement, his body reached the point where it quit sweating. He was in and out of the hospital for about a year and eventually he felt he had no other choice than to take an early retirement. He just couldn't work in that hell hole anymore. On the day he went to the personnel office to file the paperwork, the supervisor told him to hold off just a bit. Luck was shining on my dad. The supervisor found him a job in the payroll department where he worked his last five years in an air-conditioned office.

My dad was the youngest dad I knew when I was growing up, or at least he acted like it. We had a basketball hoop over our garage door in the alley, and he would play right along with the four of us boys. Most of the neighborhood kids joined in too at some point, but my dad kept up with them as well.

I think of my mom as being just a mom, but that doesn't really do her justice. She would do just about anything for my brothers and me, but she wasn't a push-over either. You couldn't sass her back – she wouldn't stand for it – which was admirable considering she barely topped the five-foot mark. She didn't work much outside the home, but she did have a job for several years as a recess monitor at Washington Elementary School. She became quite friendly with many of the teachers and on more than one occasion they even came to our house for lunch. This was a problem for me, you see, because since she knew them all that meant I couldn't get away with anything, which made my young life pretty rough at times.

All in all, I'd have to say Frank and Lorraine Rosko were good parents. They were strict but fair. We couldn't talk back, we couldn't do a lot of things, but they had their leniency to a certain degree too. They taught us right from wrong, and what more can a parent do? That was tough in a family of four boys. My brother Don is eight years older than I am, Frank (or Butch as everyone called him) was four years older than me, and then my brother Jerry came along nine years later – the typical surprise baby in the average household, I suppose.

I played sports in school. In Little League I was the catcher, despite the fact I was the smallest kid there. I even made the all-star team my first year but never got to play that game. The team practiced for a whole week, then this other kid came in from vacation and since it was his last year, the coach gave him my uniform. Go figure. After Little League I played in Babe Ruth League. My dad coached the team and I was his second baseman. I won some trophies, and our team won first place.

In high school I played freshman basketball, but my sophomore year I didn't make junior varsity. I tried out for the baseball team in my junior year but didn't make that either. Guess what happened my senior year? Right – I didn't make it then either, but as it turned out, one of the guys on the team got hurt so the coach ended up asking me if I wanted to play some ball. Up until the time I started with the team, they hadn't won a game, but afterwards we won a couple straight! It was a short streak, but I think I had a hand in it.

All my brothers were good kids, and we all got along. We each had our own friends because of the different age groups, but we were still brothers and still close. Like my brother Butch. He was a guy that everybody loved. He was just an easy-going kid who attracted fun. He liked fast cars and whatever went along with that! He played baseball with me in the summertime down at the Little League field and in the evenings we'd play basketball in the alleyway. He was always good to me, always made me proud to have him as a brother. After he graduated high school, he started work at the steel mill. My uncle had to help him get the job because my dad wanted us to stay out of the mill, but it was still good pay with good benefits for someone who didn't want to go to college. Butch needed a good job because he ended up marrying his girlfriend Dot, and before long they had a son and a baby daughter.

Either the police or the hospital called us that night – I don't remember which, but you know sometimes it just doesn't matter, and you can never recall specific details. Butch had been out driving with four other guys. He rounded a curve, somehow lost control of the car and smashed into a tree on the driver's side. The impact knocked him out of the car, but the other guys had only minor injuries. We suppose he hit his head on that tree when he was thrown, but at least he was still alive, though his head injuries were very serious. I couldn't figure out why something like that would happen to him. He was a good driver, a responsible person. Why did it happen to my brother?

Only my mom and dad went to the hospital that first night, and I stayed home with Don and Jerry. I can remember thinking he would certainly be all right. He was young - only twenty-one - he was strong too. He'd snap out of it. When I was allowed to go to the hospital the second day, I walked into his room rather stiffly, not knowing what to expect. I saw him lying in the bed. He wasn't moving, his eyes were closed, and his skin was pasty. His head was bandaged and I could see dried blood here and there. Was he going to make it? I didn't know, I couldn't tell, and no one was saying much. Maybe no one knew. My parents looked drained and pale, like they were holding back a dam about to burst. Then, I saw his head move slightly, and his eyes fluttered and finally opened. They were bloodshot and wet, and he looked around the room as though he didn't know where he was. He spoke too, rather softly but hoarsely. "Oh no, oh no," was all he said. His head fell back on the pillow and a thin sheet of perspiration was on his face. We stayed with him a while. He died the next morning.

I was seventeen-years-old, and I know now that a seventeen-year-old doesn't understand death the way an older person does. I saw how it affected my parents – they cried into the night, and I had never witnessed such sorrow. I saw how it affected his wife. She seemed lost and angry and mournful all at the same time. My brother Don took it the hardest of us boys, I think, because he knew Butch better than anybody. Jerry was only eight at the time and I don't think he realized much what was going on. I can only be sure about how I felt, and I guess it just didn't soak in that he was gone, at least not until I got to the funeral home.

I could smell the flowers before I walked through the door. It was a sweet, feminine smell that didn't seem appropriate around my brother Butch. People were telling me how sorry they were. My parents were crying again. Then I walked into the room where he lay in his casket, and I suddenly realized I was looking at him for the last time. Before then, it was like I had been dreaming and figured I would eventually wake up, but at that moment, standing there frozen and gazing down at him, I knew I never would. Seeing him hit me harder than my parents just telling me he was dead. It hurt worse than hearing the crying and seeing the tear-streaked faces. Now I saw him. It was real.

For the rest of that day, I felt everything happening around me, but I wasn't really a part of it. It was as though my emotions were being strained through a sieve and only a tiny bit could push through. What was life going to be like without Butch? My parents were concerned about his family, his children. I didn't fully understand those implications – the practical side of death – I just knew I wasn't going to see him anymore.

When I think back on losing Butch, I realize that my youth was somewhat of a cushion for me in dealing with his death. I was able to go back to school and get involved in the usual antics of a seventeen-year-old rather than focus on the loss we all suffered on a constant basis. I saved those thoughts for quiet times at home or in church. I didn't grasp how much we had all been affected or how different our family was to be without Butch around. I didn't comprehend the depth of sadness my parents felt. Losing a brother and losing a son is two different things, though I couldn't possibly understand that at the time. Even today I see the lasting effects of his loss on their faces. Some people find it hard to talk about death or the person who has died, whereas other people can talk about it even though it's painful. My parents didn't talk about it, or they would only if someone else brought it up. They went to the cemetery on his birthday or at Christmas, although we never went as a family. I learned when to talk about things and when not to talk.

My brother lived for twenty-one years, and those years made life different for all of us, just as his loss made a difference. I've always missed him and occasionally look back at the old pictures and wonder what life would have been like if he had lived. There are always things that come up that remind me of Butch, even if I try not to think of him.

He was my brother, and that's all there is.

# 5

# Janet

When you talk about love – well, everybody feels it differently I guess. Just being comfortable with Tom and wanting to be around him all the time was probably love for me. Never dramatic, never madly, wildly in love - just familiar like an old shoe.

Tom was serious about our relationship long before I was because I had to contend with my mother. Always remember that! My mother was probably the only one who didn't get along with Tom, most likely because she thought he was invading her territory by taking her daughter away. I don't think my mom wanted us kids to leave; she liked the idea of having the five of us there together. Nevertheless, my brother joined the Navy after high school and my sister went away to nursing school. I was the one who stayed home and never went far.

Tom was Catholic, too, so that of course just stirred my mother's pot even more. We belonged to the little Christian church on the corner where Mom used to teach Sunday school. We went regularly when we were little and not much after that, but we were raised to believe in God and to do the right thing. Tom's family was very active in the Catholic Church, however.

His parents were always very nice to me. His mother had a close friend – and you know how close friends can think – I have a daughter and you have a son, and they're about the same age... Well, they were trying to fix them up. Her name was Janie and he had gone to the Prom with her his senior year. Like I had gone to the Prom in my senior year with another guy, they were all pre-arranged before we got serious with each other. I remember his mother used to have Janie's picture sitting out, but I just laughed it off. I was pretty secure about our relationship.

I knew that Tom had lost his brother Butch in a car accident shortly before we met. I first heard about the accident through my brother, who was about the same age as Butch and hung around with the same group of kids. In fact, my brother saw Butch the night of the accident. Butch asked him if he wanted to go riding with them, but my brother said it was getting late so he was just going home. Then, like everybody else, we drove down the street where it happened and saw where the tree was on the curve. There was a dip in the road and they said he lost control when he hit the dip. He left a two-year-old son and a baby daughter who had Down's syndrome.

After I met Tom, he really didn't talk about the accident. His family didn't discuss sadness; they put it on the back shelf. Not like it was going to go away, they just set it aside, probably because it hurt too much. I remember Tom's mother telling me that after it happened, she took all Butch's pictures down and kept them out of sight, and I couldn't understand that. It was like they were trying to forget him or pretend he didn't exist. I really don't know how it affected Tom at the time.

Tom graduated from high school the year I met him, and he started classes at Purdue University. He wanted to be an engineer, but that didn't pan out. I think it was because he always wanted to be with me or hang out with the guys. I'm not sure if it was very hard on him when he didn't make the grades. As a twenty-year-old kid, I don't really know if you consider those life consequences. I didn't even think about it too much, and besides I always wanted him to make his own choices. It didn't seem to bother him until later in life when he saw he was getting passed over for advances and promotions.

When I graduated from high school, I quit working at the bakery and took a job at a bank. I ended up working there almost ten years. I had no thoughts of going to college; my low self-esteem kept biting me and I didn't feel I had the ability. After all was said and done and I looked back when I was about thirty, I thought I would have liked to be either a schoolteacher or an accountant. I like to work with kids – that's such a worthwhile job. As for accounting, I worked in a bank and liked numbers. I would have been happy with either.

By the time I graduated, though, Tom and I knew we were headed toward marriage. It was just going to take some time to get my mom used to that idea.

# 6

# Tom

Janet's mom was strict, dominating, and in short she didn't want Janet to date me. I never let that stop me.

Janet didn't have a high level of self-confidence because of her mother. She always kept her thumb on Janet and everybody else as well. Janet's brother and sister would stand up for themselves, but Janet never fought back. Whatever her mother wanted, that's what she did, and at times that was pretty hard for me to swallow. As time passed, though, she seemed to mellow a bit, and even with our periods of ups and downs, it wasn't anything I couldn't handle.

With Janet and me – well that was a different story. We were a match and I was very attracted to her. She had a great personality, always friendly, quiet, and kind of shy. There was nothing I didn't like about Janet.

After I graduated, I started running around with a guy who was a few years older than me, probably twenty-two or twenty-three. He had a Corvette, so of course I let him drive! We used to hang out at the gas station. The boys always hung out at the gas stations, the girls always hung out – wherever.

I did more than hang out though. I went to Purdue Calumet for engineering. Before college, I never had to study. No matter what the class, I could get good grades without ever having to crack a book, so consequently I never developed strong study habits. I'll be the first to admit I liked to hang out with the guys, not stay at home and study! Going to Purdue for engineering and not studying – well that was a sure-fire bet for bad grades. And that's what happened – I flunked out. I tried again and flunked out a second time. I ended up going back a few more times and got better grades, but I never stuck with it. By that time, my uncle had landed me a job at Inland Steel, just like he helped my brother Butch, and the mill wouldn't work around my school schedule, so I got frustrated and dropped out. I settled into working as a laborer in the steel mill, starting in January 1963.

Soon I quit driving the coupe. I was making good money so I bought a new car – a '63 Chevy Impala with a big four-speed engine for racing. (Yes, I did that.) I had it only six months when we decided to go to the auto show at McCormick Place in Chicago with Janet's brother and his wife. That day it was snowing so badly I could only go thirty miles an hour, but we finally made it late in the afternoon and parked over at Soldier Field. I pulled right next to this '62 Chevy that had a 409 engine in it – it had the 409 decals all over it. I figured, "If somebody's going to steal something, they're going to steal the 409, not mine." Well, I was wrong. We came out of the show around 10:00 PM and the 409 was still there, mine wasn't! We ended up getting home about 3:00 AM on the train. They found my car a week later on a street in Chicago – stripped. Even the little teddy bear I kept in the back window was gone. The only thing they didn't take was the Bible in the glove box!

In 1964 I joined the Army Reserves. I was in for six years and was trained as a medic. I worked everywhere – emergency rooms, surgery, patient wards. Surgery was my favorite. I had to know all the different instruments and when we went to summer camp on a military base, I was allowed to assist the nurses. I'd scrub in with the doctors and many times they'd give me a play-by-play of the procedure. That was amazing! In the ER I did everything from giving shots to taking blood to suturing. It was a real learning experience. When I look back, I wish I would have stayed in for the twenty years.

After Janet and I had been together about two years, I started thinking seriously about marriage and decided it was time to pop the question. My aunt knew this jeweler up on Maxwell Street in Chicago, and I know when you think of Maxwell Street you think about shysters, but this jewelry store had an armed guard at the front door and only allowed three people in at a time. So the jeweler asked me what price range I could handle and what style I wanted. I think Janet had told me what kind of ring she liked, but anyway I liked a particular ring and that's the one I bought.

So, one night we were sitting in my car in her driveway, talking, and I told her I had something for her. Very confidently, I reached in the glove box and took out the ring. She was surprised and hesitant. I don't think she was sure she wanted to get married. Off and on I had heard her same old story about dating other people because she had never done that. I was all she knew. So she opted not to take the ring right away. Eventually she did, but not right away. My confidence was dented – not crushed, but dented.

I took marriage pretty seriously. To me, marriage meant two people being together the rest of their lives, having a family, and fitting into society like everyone else. Today things have changed. Even marriage isn't like it used to be.

My parents had a good marriage – they still do in fact. When we finally got engaged, I'm sure they thought we should wait a while before we got married, even though they had always liked Janet. As for me, I was tired of dating and running around and knew it was time for me to settle down with Janet, even though I was only twenty. Well I don't know if I was ready to settle down, but I was ready to get married.

With Janet's mom, though, it was a different story. She was not happy we got engaged. But this time Janet stood up to her, which might really have been the first time, and told her that's the way it was going to be. Once Janet made up her mind we were going to get married, that was it. Then her mom eased up a bit.

We talked about children, too, and decided we would wait for a while. We wanted to get a good start in life and get settled into a house before children came along. We wanted stability and didn't want to struggle. We both agreed that two children would be nice, and so we planned our lives.

Today if a twenty-year-old came up to me and told me he was getting married, I'd tell him good luck. Nothing's stable today. When I went to work at Inland Steel, I knew I had a job for the rest of my life. Today it's not like that – you're lucky if you stay in one place five years. Back then there was security.

Janet also made the decision to convert to Catholicism. She felt I was more active in my church than she was in hers. I went to church most of the time; her family didn't go very often. Can you guess what her mom's reaction was?

# 7

# Janet

    Tom isn't a romantic – never was. I tell young girls today to look at their future father-in-law and they'll know what their lives will be like. Tom would do anything for me, but I have to tell him, nudge him, or basically hit him over the head with it. Surprises aren't in his nature. It's, "Oh, your birthday's coming. What would you like?" He would never select anything on his own. Maybe being raised with all boys has something to do with it, but I suppose we're both more practical than romantic.

    One day we were sitting in front of my house in his car and he pulled this engagement ring out of his glove box. I can't say his proposal took my breath away, but I don't know what I was expecting either. Anyway, I ended up not taking the ring right away. Poor Tom drove around with it for about two weeks. He was really hurt, naturally, and you can understand that. I knew I would be taking it – it was just a matter of time. It was my mother I was worried about, not any fear of marrying Tom. Where was I going to get the nerve to tell her? Everybody else knew about it already and they were happy, including my dad. So finally he offered it to me for the last time. It was, "Take it now or else!" So I took it.

    Actually, my mom didn't say too much about the engagement. She expected it eventually, I suppose, and we'd been going together for two years. So it wasn't too bad. Preparing for the wedding was an uphill battle, however, because I had made the decision to convert to Catholicism. Tom was active in his church, and I had gone as a little girl but not much since. I felt that as long as you believe in God it didn't really matter what church you went to. What compounded the issue was that my sister had already converted to Catholicism. She was in nursing school at a Catholic hospital and got acclimated to the faith through that.

My mom gave everybody trouble, though, not just Tom. Gradually, she came around to the fact that Tom and I were bound to be together, and after we were married Tom did a lot for her – just about anything she asked really. He was very good to her. After all she had put him through, his many kindnesses to her outweighed everything.

I was nineteen when we got engaged. I might have been one of the last of my friends to get engaged and definitely to get married. Not that everyone was doing it – that wasn't the reason - but it was comfortable because we were all doing the same thing at the same time. We were all friends in high school and then husband-and-wife friends afterwards. It was an easy transition to make.

Nineteen seems like an awfully young age to get married, but then it was more the norm. Now, I would really encourage girls to get an education and be self-sufficient first, only because they might need it at some point, not that they must be life-long career women. Being able to take care of yourself means a lot. You never know what life is going to hand you.

Our plans were to work and save enough money to pay for our own wedding. After we were married, we would live strictly on his check and save mine for a home, and once we were established, we could finally start a family. A comfortable house with four children is what I envisioned.

I also had my own plan. I was going to throw away all his paisley shirts. His mother must have bought every paisley shirt in town, but as my husband he wouldn't be wearing them.

# 8

# Tom and Janet

*(Author's note: The following chapter is presented as a conversation between Tom, Janet, and the reader. Tom's words are in italics, Janet's are in regular script.)*

*We finally got married on September 10, 1966, four years after we met and two years after we were engaged. Janet actually picked the date.*

September is still a pretty month. It's not real hot – I hate the heat. My brother and sister were thrilled that we were finally marrying. My dad was happy too, I'm sure.

*That's because he wanted you out of the house already.*

The wedding ended up being pretty big. My mother's family – coming from rural Southern Indiana and seeing this kind of wedding – it was nothing like they'd ever experienced before. Theirs were smaller affairs, usually with cake and punch.

*We planned the entire wedding together, though.*

We always did everything together.

*Except when you went to the Prom.*

Well, nothing's without flaw. The real question is would you do it all again?

*That's where I get into trouble! I don't think we had any problems with the wedding planning, though. Our likes and dislikes have always been well-matched.*

Tom never had much opinion on anything. There are just a certain few things in life that he has an opinion on, and then it's a definite opinion.

*I'm pretty liberal, you know.*

We tried hard not to hurt anybody's feelings or step on anybody's toes. I always worried about what everyone else thought. Like with Tom's nephew, Butch's boy, the thought was to make Grandma happy, so he was the ring-bearer. We had a little girl from my dad's side as flower girl, one of the cousins from my mom's side to stand up – things like that.

My sister and mother threw a bridal shower for us. It wasn't at the finest restaurant, just a little neighborhood hall and everybody helped make something. We probably had everything we needed by the time we got married. We weren't people who needed a lot of things – a few dishtowels, a few washcloths, that's about it.

*We had each other.*

Live on love! All our furniture we bought ourselves or got hand-me-downs. Today, girls get bedroom sets for presents!

*We had six attendants each.*

Yes, we had a big wedding party. I remember a friend of ours standing near my dad before he walked me down the aisle. He said to me, "That's not fair. You don't even look nervous." We had known each other for so long that we weren't nervous.

We were already good friends and comfortable with each other. There was no reason to be nervous.

*When I was standing in front of the church waiting for Janet to come down the aisle, I thought, "This is it! There's no turning back. Hurry up and get this over with!" She was a very pretty bride, very nice. I was excited, scared – all the emotions were in one basket. It's sure different than going to someone else's wedding!*

It moves so fast. You just go through the motions and don't remember a lot of details. We had a full Catholic mass that lasted about an hour. Afterwards we took pictures and then drove around in Don's Pontiac – all decorated of course! Then the wedding party went back to my mom's house to relax before the reception.

*I sat in the car because her mother wouldn't let me come in.*

My mother didn't do that! Stop kidding! But everything went well. It wasn't like I was worried about Tom not showing up or anything.

*We had about 150 people at the reception that evening. Many of them were friends of our parents, and we didn't know them very well but did our best to be sociable, all the while hoping they wouldn't ask us to introduce them to someone else!*

We had the old-fashioned wedding where they tie the apron on.

*Her, not me.*

My aunt made the cake. It was her wedding gift to us.

*She told us she wouldn't make a chocolate cake and that's my favorite. She said it was too hard to ice with white frosting. But she did it. The top layer was chocolate. We found out the next year on our anniversary – we kept it in the freezer.*

I think one thing that startled people at the very end of the reception – Tom didn't pick me up and carry me out, we were dancing and all of a sudden we just ran out.

*Why didn't I pick you up and carry you out?*

Those were my thinner days too, Tom, so you can't use that…

*We discussed that. I didn't think I could make it to the door with you and all that dress!*

I could just see you dropping me or tripping over the train. What a way to end the evening.

*On Monday we left on our honeymoon. We went to Gettysburg and Washington, DC. That area was just coming out of a drought, and all the time we were there, it poured!*

Once we got home, we started our life together. We had gotten our apartment before the wedding so everything would be ready. It was really large, and the rent was only $100. They never raised it in the four years we lived there. We lived upstairs from the couple we rented from. They became like grandparents to us; they really took us under their wing. They owned a landscape nursery – we lived upstairs from a nursery.

*We never had any hard adjustments to married life. I just went along with the program. I used the bathroom when it was my turn. Getting her trained to watch the same TV programs I watched – that was the hardest part. I've always been a TV nut, and she hasn't.*

You know, Tom's lost three wedding bands since we've been married. Right now he doesn't even own one. He would always wear it to work and in the mill you're not allowed to wear them on the floor, so he'd take it off and then lose it. I finally decided I wasn't buying him anymore.

*See what I have to put up with?*

I still wear my original diamond. I don't think I would ever change it. Some people nowadays trade up, but I guess we're more sentimental. Isn't that right, Tom?

*Yes, dear.*

September 10, 1966

# 9

# Janet

Tom and I were very fortunate because we found happiness at a young age. How many people are still looking for it? Our relationship didn't change much the day we were married. It was already solid and sure. I don't know if you could say we complimented each other but neither of us was stubborn or demanding in our ways. It was always a give-and-take relationship without even thinking about it and there was never a question of fairness. As the years progressed – well, things changed! Now Tom says, "Gee, she wasn't like this back then!" "Was" is the key word.

I never thought in terms of being an "ideal" wife. I just always wanted to be there when he came home, no matter what time it was. Maybe I fell asleep on the couch, but I was there with a meal waiting, whether it was breakfast or dinner. When he worked 4 to 12 and it was too late for him to eat dinner, I had snacks waiting, and of course I got up with him when it was time to go to work.

I didn't expect Tom to be "ideal" either. What is an ideal person anyway? Human beings aren't perfect. I just wanted somebody who cared for me and whose company I could enjoy. No fighting. My parents didn't fight and being around people who argued made me nervous. Of course, back then, people didn't put such demands on each other as they do now. Everything was simpler. You fell in love and got married because that's the way it happened. You let life unfold day by day and took quiet pleasure in each other.

I handled all the housecleaning and cooking. That was expected. I told Tom I would take the first thirty years, and he could take the second. Don't get the wrong idea, though. My house wasn't immaculate and I wasn't a gourmet cook. In fact, I used to joke when people said, "So-and-so's house is so clean you can eat off her floor!" I would say, "You can eat off mine too – there's probably some cookie crumbs or cereal there someplace!"

When we did our decorating, Tom's input was, "Do whatever you like." He was never very opinionated, but when I tried something he definitely did *not* like, I would hear about it. The best you'll ever get out of Tom is, "It's okay." Nothing's grand or wonderful. If he says, "Your car's okay" – well, that's the most positive comment he can muster. His vocabulary doesn't expand much beyond that. "It's okay, Janet." Well, okay then.

Tom's shift work was very difficult for both of us, but Tom would never have considered quitting the mill and venturing out. Back then a job in the mill was pretty much for life. We had both grown up with security, and at least in the mill there was security. So I adapted. I didn't rebel or demand; I was the type who swam with all the other fish in the fish pond. He tried several times to get a straight day position but there was always someone with more seniority. Many times I would come home from my job at the bank at 3:30 PM and he would be leaving to start the 4 to 12 shift. We would pass each other in our cars and wave.

Consequently, many of my evenings were spent at my mom and dad's house. Mom had gotten a job working evenings for the school system so my dad and I would share our dinner. We had some fine times, and even now I treasure those quiet hours together.

Diane and her husband Larry got married the same year that Tom and I did; I stood up in her wedding, and she was in mine. Her friendship has meant so much to me through the years. She is strong yet compassionate, and she's game for anything. Diane tells you how it is, and there's a lot to be said for that. Her husband and Tom grew close too, so that made life even better.

My ultimate goal with Tom was to become the typical middle-class American family. I wanted to have children and make a stable life for them. I would be the mom who made her kids breakfast every morning, hustled them out the door, and waited for them to get off the school bus every afternoon. Cookies would be baked, homework would be done, and each would be tucked in at night. If I had an ideal, that was it.

# 10

# Tom

Reality hit me hard once we got married. I was use to going out and running around as I pleased. After we were married, instead of having a good old time and spending a bit of money, we had to put money away for our future. Now we were paying bills and our income was going for furniture, a house, children. The days of not worrying about where the next dollar's coming from were gone. I guess that's about the biggest reality check there is.

I never expected Janet or our marriage to be perfect. I expected her to be as good to me as I was to her, and we would work everything else out, and that's the way it was. We gave what we could and helped each other along the way. You can't have the " It's my way or the highway" mentality. That never works – it's sure to be the highway. The relationship has to stretch and bend. You've got to be friends, not just lovers or husband and wife. The mutual respect has to be there.

We wanted the good life like any other couple just starting out. To make enough money where we could do what we wanted, buy what we wanted, and everything goes smooth and happy – that's the good life. That's what we worked for and hoped someday we'd enjoy. You strive for the future when you're young. When you're older, life comes around, and it's time to cash in.

Most of our early married life was smooth sailing, though. We had our spats once in a while but on the whole we always got along real well. It was a fifty-fifty relationship. Sometimes we had to do things I didn't like and sometimes we did things she didn't like, so there wasn't one person giving in all the time. I use to tell her she was the boss, but she would tell me I made a hell of an advisor.

We worked as a team, like with furnishing our apartment. Usually she would find something she liked and then take me to see it. If we both liked it, we bought it. If I didn't like, it we'd buy it anyway. She usually had a good hand at decorating. She knew what she liked and to me it didn't matter much. But there were points when I'd say, "Hey wait a minute, I don't think that's a good idea." And she listened. Or I'd say, "I like this better than that." Then we voted. She got two votes, and I got one.

Of course our life together would have been even easier had I worked straight days. Shift work was the hardest adjustment of all because many times we just passed each other. I never really thought of looking for work outside the mill. I tried getting a straight day job but somebody always owed somebody a favor and it was never me. Looking back, I regret that I didn't try harder to get a clerk's job or other position even though it didn't pay much money. I could have worked my way up from there.

At least the mill provided job security. Today, I realize it's not like that, as people get laid off or places shut down. Work ethics were different back then too. I always felt I was part of the group and had to pull my share. If I was scheduled and I called off, that would mean someone else would have to do my job. That wasn't right. I had to meet my responsibility. Same thing with marriage – that's a responsibility. You have to see it through. It's not something you're responsible for today and not tomorrow.

We both worked hard, knowing that once we had kids, Janet would quit work and stay home with them. I felt our kids needed Janet at home. That's how we would raise them because that would be best for them. Maybe that's why so many kids today go astray. Parents are too busy and don't have time for their own children, then the kids find their way into trouble – that's sad. We wanted to be proud of our kids and not have to worry about what mischief they were up to.

I fell in love with Janet and together we started a life. Everything else followed suit, one step at a time. I didn't know what kind of wife and mother she'd be, and she didn't know what kind of husband and father I'd be. We took a chance, and it paid off.

# 11

# Janet

After four years of working and saving, we finally reached the point where we could buy a house. We decided to stay in the same town as we had been living because it was close to my family and to work. Diane's brother-in-law and his wife lived in one of the new subdivisions we looked at. There weren't too many houses yet, but it seemed to be shaping up into a very nice neighborhood and something we could afford. We picked out a corner lot and decided on a two-story plan so that when Tom slept during the day, he would be away from the hubbub of the main level.

The builder worked with us and we took quite a few job credits on the house. In other words, we did the painting and the staining and finished off the family room behind the garage. That's when Tom got real handy – you learn quickly when you don't have the money to pay someone else to do the work! We found he had a natural talent, too, even though he'd never had the opportunity to do that type of work before. He was a bit of a perfectionist, however. It always took him longer to get things done, but we kept our humor and laughed about the fifteen minute jobs that took two hours! If he had to redo it, that was fine too. He had a lot more patience then than he does now!

Gradually, new families started moving in and the subdivision grew. The people that bought across the street graduated from high school with us. In fact there were quite a few people there that we knew, so it was like old home week again. It developed into a strong, familiar community, and if you needed something, you felt comfortable in asking. People were willing to help with each other's children or if I was frightened when Tom was at work, I felt at ease calling someone. There were lots of kids and all the moms stayed home – very family-oriented. We thought it would be the perfect place to raise children. Even the school bus picked kids up right on our corner. I could watch them from my window.

Even though I felt comfortable in the neighborhood, I still didn't stay by myself when Tom worked midnights. I would always think, "Now tonight I'm going to stay!" But then it was daylight and everything was perfect. When it got to be 10 or 10:30 PM I would tell Tom, "Maybe tomorrow night." I would stay at my parent's house, and then when it got light I would get up, come home, and get ready for work.

Having a home of our own meant we could finally start a family. I was fast becoming one of the "guys" because all my friends had at least one child. My sister and Diane both had a baby. I wanted to be a mom too, so of course I was ecstatic when the doctor confirmed I was pregnant.

I don't remember much about that pregnancy because a short time later I started spotting and eventually had to have a D & C. I had had a miscarriage. Something happened during the D & C and I had to have several pints of blood. Poor Tom, he was only about twenty-five, he sat there so long, patiently waiting and not knowing what was going on. No one was telling him anything. We thought it would be an in-and-out procedure with nothing to worry about. But that's all I remember about that time – the problems I had. I don't even remember telling Tom I was pregnant.

Time passed and about a year later I became pregnant again. Early in the pregnancy we went to Florida to visit his parents. I remember going into the bathroom and passing something large. I hoped I hadn't lost this baby as well, but the next time I went to the doctor, he verified I had. That was my second miscarriage.

I was quite upset, of course, that I had now lost two. I kept my fears and insecurities about carrying a baby full term to myself, and meanwhile the doctors kept reassuring me that I didn't have any physical problems that would preclude me from having a healthy child. They just felt it wasn't a "good, solid pregnancy" and nature had taken its course. It wasn't like they were saying my possibilities of having a baby were slim, so I kept hoping, dreaming, and trying.

Tom was disheartened and certainly felt bad for me, but growing up in his family they just didn't talk about things like that. Consequently we never discussed it much with each other or our families. People just accepted what happened and went about their business. My parents came to visit me the night I had the D & C but not much more, and Tom's parents stayed away for a while to allow me time to get back on my feet. Tom was patient and encouraging of course and overall we were anxious and willing to try again.

As I look back, the sadness comes with the loss. I ponder the unknown details of a life not realized – the might-have-been's. How different would my life have been had one or both survived? The miscarriages were just something that happened, and things happen for a reason I guess.

No, I don't really believe that. Not anymore.

# 12

## Tom

Janet and I had set certain goals in our life together. We had a plan and we were sticking to it, and so far things were going our way. After four years of saving for a house, we finally started building, and best of all we felt the new subdivision we chose would be the perfect place to raise a family.

The builder did a great job working with our tight budget. We couldn't afford to pay someone else to do the painting or have ceramic tile installed, so I did the work myself. We splurged a little and had hardwood floors installed upstairs - that was one plus for the house. Other than that I learned from scratch how to do all the finish work. Living in an apartment and working in the mill, I didn't have much experience, but I ended up doing the tiling, painting, paneling and even wallpapering. It turned out pretty good! Janet and I did it together. Well, she explained what she wanted and I did it – I guess that's together! Actually, she wasn't bad at painting and wallpapering. I taught her every trick I knew! We stained all the doors and varnished them, too.

We really loved that house. It was comfortable and not too big, though it seemed bigger because of the way it flowed. We had to get what we could afford and this one fit us well.

Janet and I had been attending the neighborhood church on a fairly regular basis. We missed now and then, but basically we practiced our faith and stayed close to the church. I felt strongly that religion was a part of life and through faith and devotion a person learned how to live. I had been brought up to believe in God and be in the House of God.

Once we got settled in our house we figured it was time to start a family, again according to plan. I didn't really know if I was ready to be a dad, but the first one's always an experiment, right? You don't know what to expect!

I don't even remember Janet telling me about the first pregnancy, and I can't tell you much about the miscarriage either. Even though it distressed me, I mostly felt thankful that she was okay. I'm sure it anguished her much more than me. She actually had to experience it, whereas I was standing on the outside looking in. I just felt it wasn't meant to be. Certainly we would be able to have more children, and I kept my focus on the future. We were young and had our whole lives ahead of us. Things happen. We simply had to try again.

It was maybe a year or year-and-a-half from the first miscarriage to the second. It seemed like it took Janet a long time to get pregnant. The second one hit a bit harder because now I'm thinking, "Okay, this is the second time, is she going to keep doing this?" But in the other respect, because she had already gone through it once, she knew more of what to expect. Perhaps it wouldn't be as traumatic for her emotionally. So my feelings were pulled both ways. Yes we understood what was going on, but were we doomed to failure?

We kept on trying. We planned for two children about four years apart, somewhere in that range. I remember talking that over and Janet wanted them spread apart more than I did. She had a set idea, maybe because that's how it was in my family with my brothers.

Thinking about the miscarriages today doesn't really stir any emotions in me. What was, was, and what is, is, and there's nothing I can do about it. I have enough problems today without creating more from the past, and with the miscarriages the children weren't personified yet to me. I didn't know them, didn't hold them, and didn't raise them. I don't even think about them now. It was hurtful and depressing, but maybe there was a reason. There had to be a reason. There always is, isn't there?

# 13

# Janet

Needless to say, when I became pregnant the third time I was a little apprehensive. I certainly didn't want this one to end in a miscarriage too. The fact that I kept spotting for a couple of months after the doctor confirmed I was pregnant didn't help matters much, even though he didn't seem overly concerned about it. I guess he just thought it would work itself out. Luckily, it did.

Tom and I had been waiting for this for seven years. I remember coming home from the doctor to tell him I was pregnant, but of course we already had our suspicions and the doctor merely confirmed it. Our families were thrilled too. My family especially was hoping for a girl – they had no granddaughters but by that time had three grandsons. Tom's side had four granddaughters but only one grandson, so I don't know what they were hoping for! But my family was definitely looking for a girl, especially my brother Chuck. He begged for a little girl! As for Tom, I don't think it really mattered. We just wanted a healthy baby. With Tom's brother having had a Down's syndrome baby, we knew we couldn't take for granted that every baby is going to be born healthy.

As time went by and my spotting stopped, my apprehension was replaced with real excitement. We were going to have a baby – finally! I never even had morning sickness, just a little queasiness from time to time. I remember being very tired; I would come home from work and just fall asleep, but that's pretty normal. I was an old mother by then, remember, according to the standards of the early '70s. I was twenty-seven! I told Tom the nurses wouldn't know whether to put me in geriatrics or OB. My roommates at the hospital ended up being about the same age, but they were on their third or fourth baby. Here I was just having my first.

We dilly-dallied with names. Then one day my sister and I were driving down the street, and it just hit me, "Oh! Jill, Jill Suzanne!" From there on out, I always called her Jill, always talked to her as being Jill Suzanne. Of course this was before we knew for sure she was a girl! She could have been a boy and I was calling *him* Jill Suzanne all that time! Luckily, Tom didn't have any problem with the name I picked out. With me, it just clicked.

I chose Raggedy Ann and Andy to decorate her room. We didn't get elaborate. We used a second-hand crib from our neighbor next door, and I bought a new mattress and new crib pads with Raggedy Ann and Andy on them. My sister-in-law painted a lamp for me and in fact I still have that. My mother-in-law makes Raggedy Ann dolls, so certainly some of those were in the room too. Even the trashcan was Raggedy Ann!

Diane's sister-in-law, the one that lived across the street from us, gave me a very nice shower. She had it at her house with all my friends and neighbors. I received all the usual gifts, even cloth diapers because that's all we used back then. My aunt also planned a small baby shower for me but that year everybody was getting either the flu or bad colds. I ended up getting the flu and the doctor wouldn't let me out of the house. So Tom, like the stand-up guy he is, substituted for me at the baby shower. He helped open the gifts with my aunts and did a great job. We even received a beautiful pink and white knit dress from my sister-in-law, who was positive I was having a girl!

My due date was the middle of January. Jill Suzanne was born January 31. Although I labored a long time, it wasn't a hard labor, just flows and ebbs. If that weren't my first baby I would have known not to go to the hospital so early! We left for the hospital about 7:30 in the morning; she wasn't born till 7:30 or 8:00 that night. They told me when I checked in it was going to be slow going, so I just laid there and watched TV with Tom, which we could easily have done at home. After dinner they put an IV in and started a medication to speed things along. That did it! I quickly got to the point where I just wanted to get it over with!

Tom did fine through labor, though. He watched TV, which is his favorite pastime anyway. No other relatives came to the hospital. We didn't call them because we didn't want everyone to be on pins and needles. That plan backfired on us, however. I figured if they called us at home they would just think we went out, but then we were gone so long they were really getting concerned. They eventually called the hospital to see if we had checked in. And sure enough…

Jill was a little thing – about 6 pounds 12 ounces, probably 20 inches long. She had a definite resemblance to the Rosko's. She had squinty little eyes and pitiful dark brown hair. You know - a lot of it and it stood straight out. In fact, years later, my sister was working in the neonatal unit and called to say they had a little girl in there that looked just like Jill! All that hair – it became her trademark! Everyone asked me if I had heartburn with the pregnancy – remember that old wife's tale – but I didn't. You couldn't even put a little bow in it. That hair was just wild.

I didn't breast feed. I can remember the nurse asking me about it in the delivery room – before they give you that shot to dry up the milk. I said, "Well, I'm not sure, what do you think?"

She answered, "Lady, you've had nine months to think about this!" Obviously she wasn't going to be very patient!

"I won't!" I replied. An instant decision.

I wasn't afraid to go home with her. I was ready to be a mom and comfortable and anxious to start our life together. We were finally a family.

# 14

# Tom

I figured sooner or later there was going to be a baby in our lives. I wasn't nervous about it, that's just the way I figured it.

When the doctor verified Janet was pregnant, I sure was happy. In fact, I took her out to celebrate. We went to a nice restaurant and had an all-you-can-eat chicken dinner. The waitress asked what kind of potatoes we wanted, and I was never much of a French-fry eater, but all of a sudden I had a huge craving for French fries. I ate three big plates of French fries that night and I've eaten them ever since.

To me, it didn't matter if it was a girl or a boy. I think at the time I would have liked one of each, but I didn't have a preference as to which came first.

The delivery was really something! You know how you see in the movies where the woman is pregnant and it's time for her to go to the hospital, so she wakes up her husband and they jump in the car and drive like crazy? Well, when our big day arrived Janet woke me up and we packed all the bags in her little Mustang. I got ready to tear out of the driveway and she said, "No, you just drive the speed limit." Drive the speed limit! That hurt.

Once we got to the hospital, it took a long, long time - eleven hours I think. We sat there in the labor room and watched TV all day. Nothing exciting. Occasionally she would moan a little bit. It got tiring after a while, but that's what we did for eleven hours. I wanted to go out and get a hamburger or something, but Janet wouldn't let me.

When it finally came time to deliver, they whisked her into another room and ushered me into the father's waiting room. After what seemed like hours, the door finally opened and the doctor and nurse walked in. I couldn't take my eyes off the tightly wrapped bundle the nurse was carrying. Smiling, she said, "This is your daughter." She unwrapped her a little for me to see. She seemed so tiny, and I remember she was crying, probably because they bothered her with the unwrapping. I held her for just a few minutes before they took her to finish cleaning her up. I'm sure she was cute, but I don't remember specifics. Did she have hair? I don't recall.

Janet was fine and everyone was very, very happy. I didn't send Janet flowers or anything like that – maybe I should have. No, she should have sent me flowers! I was under more stress than she was! She just had to lie in bed. I was the one who sat there for eleven hours! (Yes, I'm kidding.)

Oh, I do remember that we had gone out and bought a new car before Jill was born. We bought a 1973 Monte Carlo – very sharp. It just happened to come in at the same time Jill was born and the salesman called for me to pick it up. Now that was the exact day I had to pick up Janet and Jill from the hospital. Janet said to come get them first so they could get settled in at home before I went to get the new car. I didn't think that was a good idea, so I went to pick up the new car first. I thought it would be special to pick them up in a brand new car! Boy, I never lived that one down. Everyone chided me that I got my new car before my new daughter.

Fatherhood hit home. There was constantly something to do, and she cried quite a bit at first. Babies always have their days and nights mixed up. I don't know what it is but they want to stay up all night and sleep all day. That's what Jill did, and our first priority was to get that turned around. Once we did that being a dad wasn't too bad.

# 15

# Janet

I guess Tom told you how he had to go pick up the new car before he picked us up at the hospital. He got teased about that for a long time. When she was older even Jill would taunt, "Yeah, dad had to go get his new car before he came and got me!" Anyway, we made it home. I dressed Jill in a green and white sweater and blanket that a good friend of ours had knitted. She looked so tiny and precious.

We were very excited. We had this new baby and she was healthy! So many good things, so much love in our lives. Of course we were a little nervous but meeting the demands of an infant wasn't a tough adjustment. Yes, after seven years of marriage we were settled into our routine, but we were still flexible enough to enjoy every minute with her. We just rolled with it.

I was always tired, naturally, and had to develop a schedule. I quit work but never missed it. She kept me busy! For the most part I was on my own. I remember when we came home from the hospital, Diane and my sister showed me how to work the sterilizer and my mother-in-law came over one day and did my laundry, but other than that, it was just Tom and I.

My dad used to come over in the evenings when Tom was working 4 to 12 and my mom was at work too. I spent a lot of time with him after Jill was born. Remember my dad was not the type of person that got short or upset, but during those evenings while I was warming up the bottle and Jill would start to cry, he would get very agitated with me! Then I always got the bottle too hot and would have to cool it down, which took more time, and of course neither he nor Jill appreciated that!

Jill was a good baby. She was a sleeper; I don't know where she got that from. She didn't even have her days and nights mixed up. During the night when she woke up, Tom would warm the bottle and I would feed her. She always fell asleep as I rocked her – on her tummy! That's what I remember about her as an infant. And her wild hair – like Raggedy Ann!

Tom was doing fine with fatherhood. He wasn't big on doing anything hands-on; he didn't feel at ease when she was small. He claimed he was afraid he'd drop her or inadvertently hurt her. He blossomed when she started to play with him, though. I think a lot of men are like that, at least they were back then. He would hold her, sure, but I would do the care. That was a woman's job. Women today are probably thinking, "Boy is she off target." But that's how it was – you didn't expect fathers to do much actual care. He was always willing to try anything I asked, but he gave me moral support more than anything else.

So mostly it was just Jill and I, all the time. When she was an infant, I remember there were a couple of occasions where my mother-in-law babysat with her for a while. Jill cried and cried the whole time. She told me Jill must have had a stomachache or something, but my sister-in-law said, "No, she just misses her mom." One night my brother, who loved my daughter dearly, told us he would babysit for her so we could go to my ten-year high school reunion meeting. Well, he was never so glad to see our car pull up in his whole life, as she had cried the entire time. "Unbelievable" is what my mother-in-law said. She had raised four children, and she couldn't believe that missing me would be a reason for a child to cry like that at such a young age.

She crawled before she walked; I remember her pulling up on everything. Our family room was one step down from the kitchen, and I always kept that padded because it was ceramic tile, so if she rolled backwards she wouldn't hit her head. She crawled all over. She must have walked at about a year – she was just a short little thing.

Her first tooth came in when she was close to a year, too. At the time Tom's brother needed someone to lend a hand in moving him to Oklahoma, so Tom and I helped out. Jill stayed with our family, and she cut her tooth while we were away. I was heartbroken I missed that – her first little tooth.

When she was a toddler my brother bought her a Big Bird doll. She took it to bed with her every night – she loved her Big Bird! She held it by the neck. She had a favorite blanket and a pacifier too, and I still have the doll she used to carry around. That's probably the only thing that had worse looking hair than Jill when she was little! She also loved to play with purses. When the grandmothers came over, she would drag their big purses all around the house.

Once she got over her fear of being away from me, she grew to love people and became very sociable. She adored other kids and was more than willing to be in crowds – quite outgoing. That's where I think she took more after Tom. She wasn't afraid of anything and would try almost everything!

When her daddy was there, he came first. He carried her everywhere. My mother-in-law would say, "Put that baby down, she can walk." Well, he wouldn't do that. She wanted to be held, and he held her. She loved Tom, and they played as often as his work schedule allowed. As soon as she talked and walked and displayed her personality, she basically wrapped him around her little finger. I felt so warm watching him lay on the floor as she crawled all over him.

I liked to read her the Disney books. I read Thumper a lot because that was my favorite! It had a rhyme to it and it just flowed. I didn't play with her all the time; I felt she had to learn to entertain herself, too, and not always be demanding of other people's attention. When I did play with her, we played quieter games or watched *Sesame Street* so she could see Big Bird.

Jill and I used to spend the night at my mom's when Tom worked midnights. My old fears were ever present right over my shoulder, and I still hated when Tom wasn't home. My mom had a double bed and Jill would sleep with me. In the morning she would scamper out of bed and my father would already be up cooking breakfast, the usual fried eggs and toast. Jill would climb on his lap and eat breakfast with him – a bite for her and a bite for him! Eventually I did make the transition to stay home at night, probably when Jill was about three. I always felt guilty for dragging her around like that.

I recall one evening when she was still a toddler and Tom was working 4 to 12. There was a small restaurant in town, and she and I went there for dinner and played "big girls." I sat on one side of the booth, and she sat on the other, and we had supper together. She was so proud and acted so grown up.

I had waited many years to share an evening like that. I was living my dream.

# 16

# Tom

It didn't require much of an adjustment for Janet and me to be parents because we had planned for it for so long. It wasn't all of a sudden – boom – out of the clear sky. When you plan for something and when you're surprised by something are two different situations. Not that it was easy – families are never easy. You have to work to have a good family, but it wasn't bad. Of course Janet did most of the work. I didn't know about kids, I knew about steel mills and steel mill work. That was my end of it.

I did almost everything for Jill except I wasn't a pants-changer. I delegated that to Janet. I'd feed her the bottle, but when it came to feeding her solid food that wasn't my bag either. I didn't have the patience to feed her like that. You know you're supposed to taste it first? I don't think so! I watched her when Janet slept, cleaned house a bit, went to the grocery store, and cooked some of the meals. I washed the new car, took it for a ride, and made sure it didn't freeze up! Didn't want any problems there. I did what any other new dad would do, I guess.

Jill was a real daddy's girl. Anytime we'd go someplace she'd want me to hold her constantly. She would hold out her arms for me to pick her up, and I would just automatically do it. Her first word was daddy, too.

As a baby she had bronchial pneumonia, and it scared the life out of us. Janet even had to rock her rather than laying her down, she was so congested. Her temperature reached 105 so the nurse told us to put her in a bathtub with cool water and you think, "Do I really want to do that?" Well, we did it and it worked. She had that two winters in a row and then she came out of it, thank God.

She had a bimby – that was her blanket. I think it was white with satin around the edges. She also had a big yellow bird she carried for quite a while. Then of course there was her teddy bear. My mom had to re-sew that because the face and feet were falling off after so long.

We took a trip to Disney World when Jill was about three-years-old. My parents always go down there for the winter, and we went to visit them. She loved Mickey Mouse, probably from watching him on TV. Anyway, once we got in the park the first character we saw was Donald Duck, and he came over and posed for a picture. He talked to her and even leaned down to kiss her, but instead he hit her nose with his bill and she cried and cried. That didn't go over too well. We finally got her to stop crying, but she didn't want any part of those animals anymore – till she saw Mickey Mouse. Once she saw him, everything was fine again.

Actually, we went down to Florida four or five years straight, I think. We drove, although one time we flew. Poor Janet's knuckles were stark white, she was grabbing the arms of the seat so tight.

# 17

# Janet

My dad was diagnosed with colon cancer when Jill was only about two-years-old. He endured surgery, chemotherapy, radiation, and also had a colostomy. After a year of fighting, it finally overtook him.

Early in March, 1976, he was fairly stable, and Tom and I were thinking of going down to Florida with Tom's parents for a couple of weeks. My dad encouraged us to go, saying he was doing okay and didn't want us staying home in all that Indiana cold. So we went, but we called every day. One day they told me he was admitted to the hospital.

We started back home, coming as fast as we could. When we at last reached his house, the neighbor met us and said it didn't look good and we should probably go straight to the hospital. He died just a few days later.

We were all there at the hospital when he actually passed away and had just gone to phone some of the other relatives who wanted to see him before he died. We heard them call a Code Blue on the loud speaker and like a piercing arrow we knew instinctively it was for him. That was March 22. He had been conscious up until the end. I remember him trembling he was so cold, and his skin felt lifeless even before he passed. He had hemorrhaged internally.

I never really got a chance to talk to him much before he died. I think I shunned anything beyond light conversation because I was trying so hard to keep my own emotions under control. I didn't want to upset him so I was always restrained, like, "Hi Dad, how are you? Are you feeling better?" I thought if I talked about his disease or about death I would depress both him and my mother, so I evaded it for all our sakes. I know there are some people who can sit and really talk – like a husband and wife, if they know one is terminal, they talk about what they want with the kids or the future or their care. They have a need to iron things out. But I didn't think my dad was in any condition for that so it was pretty much, "Hi Dad. Love you, Dad."

During the year he had been sick, my mom had time to get used to the possibility he could be terminal. So she did alright although I'm sure it was difficult, especially when she started spending all those days and nights in the hospital, waiting. The cancer had started to spread and things just got harder and harder. She became more anxious and upset. We were always around her, though, my brother and sister and I.

It was traumatic for her when he actually died. I don't think she was too concerned about her own future. She knew the three of us were always there at her call – whatever she needed financially or physically. If she didn't want to be alone one of us would go stay with her, or she would stay with us. She never had to face those worries, although she didn't seem to mind being alone very often. Their house was paid for so she opted to stay there. She tried to be independent, but of course she really wasn't. Yes, she was able to live alone and keep her own home, but she didn't mow the lawn or do general maintenance. We all helped out. She still drove and even found a job for herself. A local bank that had a little cafeteria hired her to do their cooking, and she continued on with that for quite a while. So she kept herself busy.

Eventually, my brother ended up moving in with her. He was divorced and living in an apartment so it was convenient for him. After that, his two sons from a previous marriage came to live there too. My brother, who had been living the single life for some time and was used to coming and going as he pleased, had to make the transition to being a full-time dad again. It was wonderful for my mom, and she became a real constant to those boys. She gave them stability – they knew that she would always be there to get them up for school and when they came home dinner was on the table and their clothes were clean. So the four of them lived together until the boys were old enough to go on their own.

My dad retired when he was sixty-two, due mainly to his health. I remember he got only one social security check before he died, after working all those years. He worked since he was seventeen – all his life.

# 18

# Tom

Janet's dad was such a good man. When he passed away, it was hard on everybody.

Janet was trying to be strong throughout the year he was ill, although naturally she constantly worried about him. After his initial surgery we all thought he was improving and it was devastating to find out otherwise. At the end Janet was very distraught, as was everyone else. Overall, though, I was surprised at how well she actually got through it. He had been battling the cancer for a year and during that time we all had a chance to get used to the idea that it could be the end for him.

I was in the room with him right before he died. He was awake and alert but wasn't talking very much – just small talk. I saw his eyes turn serious and almost desperate, and he asked me to go get Janet's mom. He got rather abrupt with me when I didn't go right away, but then I took another look and realized how ashen his skin had become. I quickly went to find her, and just a little while later he passed away.

Initially, it was hard for Janet's mom. She was alone and had to make ends meet, which she never had to do before. He had always paid the bills and did all the bookwork, but now that fell to her. Janet and I were there quite a bit, so she had us to look out for her as well as Betty and Chuck. If she ever needed anything, Janet was there, and eventually life settled into a routine again. I was still working shift work, of course, and so Janet spent a lot of time at her mom's. They leaned on each other, and that was fine with me.

# 19

# Janet

I guess I'm just not a real baby-maker. We intended to have our children two years apart but best-laid plans never seem to work out. I was confident it would eventually happen, though, and sure enough when Jill was three-years-old the doctor confirmed I was pregnant with our second child.

Tom and I suspected I was pregnant so it really wasn't a big shock to him when I came home with the news. When we made the announcement to the rest of the family, they were all happy, of course, but by that time my brother and sister as well as Tom's brothers all had children so it wasn't earth-shattering like the first or second grandchild. My friend Diane was actually pregnant at the same time. It was her second child too, and she was due six weeks behind me.

I think this time we were hoping for a little boy; it's nice to have one of each. Jill wanted a big sister but of course that wasn't going to happen since she was the oldest! She was excited about the pregnancy – she used to pat my stomach and feel the baby move, keeping her eyes peeled for an arm here or an elbow there!

Having a baby meant Jill got to move up to the bigger bedroom. She helped decorate it all in pink – she loved pink. We decided on Strawberry Shortcake from the Spiegel's catalog and I ordered the entire set – curtains, bedspreads, the whole nine yards. That was her first "big girl" room, and then as time went on she outgrew Strawberry Shortcake and moved into the "ruffle" stage. We also redecorated the nursery in clowns and balloons.

I didn't have any problems during this pregnancy like I had with Jill, although I probably had more morning sickness. In fact I had a frog that sat on my kitchen sink that had a really big mouth to hold a scrubbing pad. I couldn't even look at that frog with something in its mouth! That just didn't sit well with my stomach! I gained weight fast, I remember. My friends said it looked like I was going to have twins, and when I told the doctor that, he started wondering too. He ended up ordering an x-ray that proved there was only one. He was noticeably relieved, and I guess we were too!

May 8, 1977, was Mother's Day and we were supposed to go to my in-laws. We never made it because I woke up that morning in labor. We called my in-laws to tell them not to expect us, and they offered to come get Jill. She was packed and ready to go. My father-in-law was so nervous, however, he almost left without taking her clothes. I shoved her little suitcase in his hand at the last minute!

We arrived at the hospital and my doctor was already there. He said it was going to be a long time so we just sat back to play the waiting game again, and then all of a sudden I got nauseated. The hard labor kicked in almost immediately. It felt like those battering rams you see in the old movies – the big wooden gate and they're beating against it. Let me out! Let me out! The nurse called the doctor and told him I was going fast, but when she came back, she told me even though he was on his way back to the hospital he didn't believe her. So the nurses had another doctor standing by and in fact he was already in the delivery room with me when my doctor showed up just in time to deliver our son. I remember him teasing Tom that he wasn't going to have to mow the lawn anymore because now he had a little boy.

My total labor was only about three or four hours. He was 8 pounds, 12 ounces, and long too. I always called him my little moose. Jill was so tiny when she was born, and this one just looked huge! He looked exactly like Tom, too. When you walked past the nursery, you just knew that was a Rosko baby.

Picking his name took a while. We laughed all through the pregnancy because he was just "baby." Not like Jill Suzanne! Just no-name baby. Tom's full name is Thomas Joseph, and I really wanted a Joseph in there. I had thought about Jeffrey Joseph or Michael Joseph. We were in the hospital before we really came to terms with it and made a decision for the birth certificate, and then we decided it would be Jeffrey Alan! Tom wasn't too keen on Joseph, and with his initials being JAR, I just called him my baby JAR.

My in-laws came to the hospital to see him, and I told my mother-in-law she would have no trouble picking out which baby was her grandson. She didn't, either! When my brother came to see him the first time, he brought him a little Mustang – a boy toy. Who would have known he'd grow up loving Mustangs!

I was ready to go home. It was during the week and Tom was working days, so I asked him if he minded if my brother Chuck took me home instead of waiting for him to get off work. So that's what we did, and my brother brought Jill along, too. She came in the hospital and picked us up; she was only four-years-old at the time. I got in the car and held Jeff in my arms (that's what we did in those days) and Jill sat between my brother and I. Oh! She was just so excited! I wish Tom had been there to see that. "Mom! Can I see his feet? Let me see the feet!" My brother and I, watching her, had tears in our eyes. She was so thrilled over this new baby; she couldn't wait to get home to hold him. She was his little mama, and she stayed thrilled, too, right up until the time Jeff started getting into her toys.

# 20

# Tom

I didn't have any cravings when Janet was pregnant with Jeff, but I still liked French fries.

This time I wanted a boy so we'd have one of each. It didn't matter to me if this was the last baby or not – we could have had one or two more. But after going through what we did for Jill – it took such a long time to get pregnant, and then I had to wait so long through the delivery – I figured this might be the last.

Her pregnancy was easy. No major problems that I remember. I'm sure we redecorated the nursery, and I know we moved Jill to the bigger bedroom. I think Jill was too young to be excited about the new baby; I don't think she fully realized what that meant.

These are things I don't remember much about. I don't know why I don't remember, but I sure don't. They are like vague pictures in my mind that I try to grab as they drift past, and sometimes I'm successful and other times I'm not, like with names for the baby. I know we talked about them, and once again Janet had two votes and I had one. We ended up with Jeffrey Alan and I did like that one.

It wasn't as exciting bringing Jeff home from the hospital as it was with Jill. There was no new car! We settled in nicely, though. We were pros already because we'd gone through it once before. The second time around isn't nearly as traumatic as the first, with the nervousness and uncertainty. He was a good baby, too, which I'm told makes a big difference. Oh, he had his days and nights mixed up a tad, but we got him straightened out quickly enough because we had learned from Jill. Poor Jill – the first one is always the test case. With the second one you're always a little more lenient, too. You're not apt to get flustered or frustrated as quick. You always want your kids to be perfect, but then nobody's perfect.

Jill did fine with Jeff. At first, Jill was a little – well, I guess jealous because she was used to me picking her up and carrying her all over. Now I was carrying him, and she didn't like that very much, but that didn't last long. She was getting older anyway and too big to carry around – four-years-old! That was probably the only instance of jealousy, though, and other than that she was very pleased with him. She loved holding him, and Janet would sit her on the couch and hold Jeff on Jill's lap so he didn't fall or get hurt. She would wrap her little arms around him and be all smiles and giggles.

All in all it wasn't much different having two children instead of one. No major difference raising a boy compared to a girl either, at least in the early years! I don't feel I really raised the kids – Janet did most of that. I was the breadwinner. Our house was established, and my purpose and goal was to keep it running smooth. Janet stayed home and raised the kids. We were fortunate to be able to do that. When both the man and the wife have to work, you don't have enough family time. The kids are left to do for themselves and everyone suffers because of it. You need that cohesive, stable environment because in the long run it makes a difference.

# 21

# Janet

As soon as I brought Jeff home from the hospital, my neighbor came over and brought a little boy outfit for him to wear. I remember her saying she did *not* want to see him in any little girl hand-me-downs. A lot of people brought over boy outfits for the same reason, I think! As time went on, though, I really didn't see much difference between raising a girl and a boy. I felt it was mainly a difference in their personalities rather than their sex having much to do with it. I had one friend who said, "Oh my God, I don't know what I'd do if I had a little boy – they're always so naughty!" I don't know about that – there are plenty of naughty girls out there, too!

Jill was a little mother to Jeff. When he was a few months older, she would help me by holding the bottle. I was right there with her, though, always concerned about choking, you know! Because Tom was still working shift work, the kids and I were alone often. We bonded very closely to each other and whatever we did, it was always the three of us. Jill never minded this. She never showed any signs of jealousy until they got much older, maybe in junior high. But as small children she let him come along with her friends without a problem – until he reached the point where he started developing his own opinions about things. You know kids. They blend for a while, and then there are those years where they un-blend. Most of the kids in the neighborhood were girls, but they played with Jeff until he started deciding for himself what he was and wasn't going to do. Then they figured it was time to leave him alone!

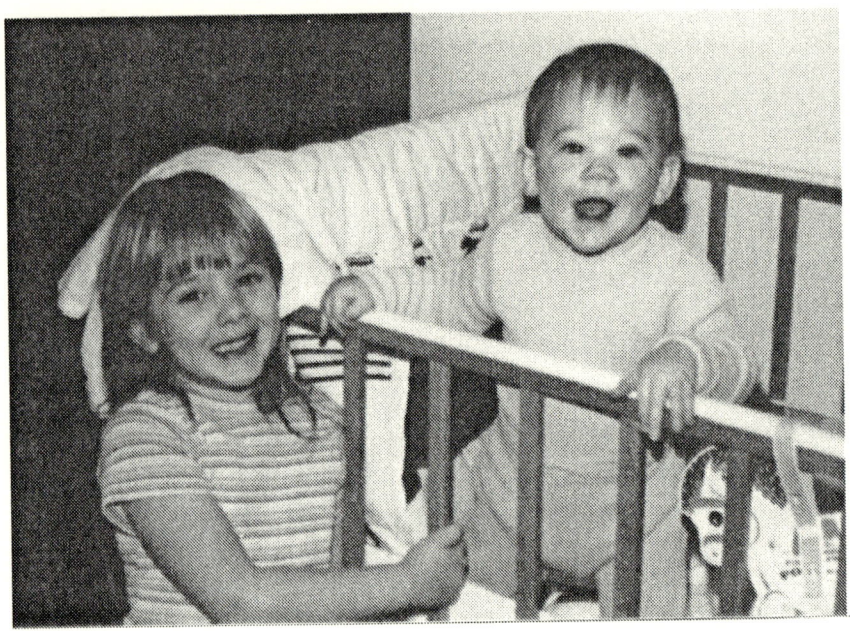

Jill Age 5, Jeff Age 1

Before long Jill was starting kindergarten. She was so eager to go to school! It wasn't like she was hanging on my leg afraid to let go. She was the first one on the bus! I cried of course, but she didn't. She was so excited to get out there with the kids.

Jeff Age 3, Jill Age 7

As Jeff grew to the pre-school years, he was still very quiet and easy-going, but he definitely had his own mind, like the times I would take him to Story Hour at the public library. He agreed to go in the library, but when it came time to go to the story room, he just wasn't going to budge. That was how he worked, and he was like that his whole life. He would go along with you until it got to a certain point, and then it was no, he didn't want to do that. He didn't throw any tantrums or fits; he just knew what he did and didn't want to do, and that was that.

The same thing would happen at Halloween. Jill would be so thrilled – she was going to be this or that. We decided what Jeff was going to be and he would stand there quietly while we put on his costume and make-up, but when it was time to leave the house, he resolved he wasn't going anywhere looking like that and he would take it all off and go in his regular clothes. He would let us fuss all over him, but we knew it was only going to go so far.

Maybe he thought he was just letting me have my fun, and then he would step in and say that's enough.

I remember one time when he was still very little, my neighbor Carol and I were sitting in the family room and he was upstairs taking his nap. Carol and I must have been talking and got distracted. Remember we had a two-story home, and you could walk downstairs from the bedrooms right out the front door. Well Jeff did just that. My God, I was panic-stricken. I had all the neighbors looking for him. Then we walked around to the side of the house, which bordered another neighbor's house. There sat Jeff on this little school bench the neighbor had decorating her porch. Exasperated, I said, "What are you doing!" He shrugged and said he was waiting for Peter to come home to play with him.

Jill Age 8, Jeff Age 4

Another time when he was only three or four my sister was babysitting for him. There was a big retention pond about a block or two away from her house. My mom was there too that day. My mom and sister were chatting away and then my sister went to check on Jeff. She couldn't find him. She looked all over the house and called for him, but he didn't answer. She was so frightened chills were running up her spine. They immediately ran off to check the pond. When they got back they found him sitting behind the sofa, and he just wasn't going to answer. My sister was so upset she could barely speak. He had that stubborn streak way back then.

He was shy, too, except when we would go over to my sister's house and he knew they kept the cookies on the shelf in the pantry. He would just walk over to the pantry like he owned the place and help himself to those cookies. I told him, "No, Jeff, you don't do that." My sister would say, "That's okay, that's what they're there for." He always went right for them.

I remember his first day of school. I think he would rather have stayed home. I took him along with a little neighbor boy and his mom and as soon as the boys got preoccupied in the classroom my neighbor whispered, "Let's make a break for it before they realize we're gone!" So we did, and after that he liked school. He did very well and rarely missed a day. Whenever I went for a parent conference, the teacher would say he associated well with everybody. He just went with the program.

In first grade he rode the bus with his sister. They were usually together, and I think he relied on her a lot. She was the leader. I always wondered if that's why he didn't talk as much or wasn't as expressive verbally. She did everything for him and overshadowed him. They didn't really start nitpicking and bickering with each other until she got into junior high and he was in the late elementary years, and then he became the pesky little brother in her eyes.

Jill was as easy-going as Jeff was strong-willed. She was like me; she didn't buck the establishment. She was also very social – just a butterfly. She liked parties, loved her birthday, and adored my sister's son Brian. When I would babysit Brian, she was so happy because she had a friend. We would go out in the yard and play the day away.

All three of us used to bake cookies together, especially around Christmas. We all favored eating the raw dough. Tom couldn't believe that we'd eat it like that, but we did! So it wasn't the end product – it was the making that we enjoyed!

Discipline was not much of a problem. With Jill all you had to do was pull the paddle out from under the cabinet just to scare her – that's all it took. She was brave about most things, except that paddle!

Jill was in Brownies and then Girl Scouts, and I was the troop assistant. Because Tom would be working, Jeff would always come along for the meetings. It never bothered him. The leaders always gave him something to do that wasn't "girlie." None of the other girls had brothers, so he was the one and only. He even went to Brownie camp with us.

Jill's First Communion, Age 8

After Tom and I got married, we really didn't go to church routinely. We knew in our hearts that we should, but we'd get up Sunday morning tired from the week and decide we'd just go the next week. It gets easier and easier to say, "We'll sleep in today."

After the kids were born and baptized, we took our responsibilities more seriously. Both Jill and Jeff went through all the Catholic education. Every Wednesday night was CCD. Sometimes I had to wonder if they were learning anything, though. Jill took it pretty much to heart – she was easy, but with Jeff it was, "Why do I have to be here?" He would horse around, although once in a while he'd surprise me. We'd be driving down the street and something would come out of his mouth about Jesus or God, and I would think, "Oh my, he must have been listening!"

I don't believe you have to go to church to be a good person or to believe in your chosen faith. I had always worshiped God and prayed for health and safety. Just because you sit in the first pew in church every Sunday doesn't make you the better person. There are people who never go to church who go out of their way to do good for someone else. That's their nature, that's how they were raised, and that's how they believe.

I do think structured religion is best, however. I used to tell my priest I sit on the fence about a lot of things. He would say one day I was going to fall off that fence, and I'd have to fall one way or the other. I guess I see religion not as Catholic, Baptist, Protestant, or any particular sect. I just see it as being a good person, having a good heart, and trying to do your best. No one is perfect without disappointments or frailties.

Sometimes it was a real challenge to get through church services with two children, however. I remember one Sunday in particular. I don't recall what Jill actually did during church, but understand I have to really get pushed to get perturbed. She must have pushed my button just right that morning because I led her out to the foyer to give her a good talking to. One of the ushers saw me coming and stood there in the corridor waiting for me. He kept talking and talking until mass was over, so I never did get to scold her! That day she was lucky.

# 22

# Tom

Jeff was more of a homebody than Jill, so when his first day of school rolled around, he wasn't nearly as excited as she had been. I think he enjoyed school once he got there, but he would have preferred to stay home with Mom. Even so, he was a good student and a quick learner. He took after his father! At times homework was a problem because he really didn't have to do it – he could wing it. The only time he'd get in trouble was when it had to be written out, and then I was always after him to get it done, but as a whole he could sleep through class and still do well.

Jill, on the other hand, had to work at her grades. Math wasn't her forte and it was a rough battle for her. I'm sure it bugged her that Jeff could breeze through so easily. She studied hard, always did her homework, and Jeff got better grades without trying.

Our kids were very fortunate growing up. We had a swing set and a swimming pool in the backyard, and of course that meant the neighborhood kids were also in the yard, but we liked it that way. We could keep an eye on our own! Jill and Jeff both learned to swim. Jill really loved it, and Jeff was lukewarm. She could swim!

We went on several family vacations too. In Florida we'd stay in my parent's pop-up camper, then they bought a trailer and we switched to that. We enjoyed staying at the campground. At night we'd huddle around the campfire, and during the day we'd bum around or take in the usual sites, like Disney World and Cape Canaveral. When the kids got a little older, we visited the Smokey Mountains in Tennessee and also Colorado where Janet's cousin lived. Jill and Jeff both loved traveling. Of course, we drove everywhere – Janet and flying don't mix!

I think Jill mostly took after me. She had an adventurous spirit, craved excitement, and was more than willing to take risks. Jeff, on the other hand, was more like Janet – very quiet and less ambitious about getting out and doing things. He enjoyed sports and would actively participate, but around people he wasn't as social as Jill. If we had company, Jill would be right in there conversing with everybody, whereas Jeff would sit and watch TV, speaking only if someone spoke to him first. I usually managed to coax Jeff into attempting whatever Jill and I were doing, however. I actually took them both horseback riding and tobogganing a couple of times, or we'd go swimming. Jill swam underwater like a fish.

Jill's feelings would bruise very easily whenever we had a disagreement. She would sulk alone in her room, but once she got settled down we could reason with her. Jeff wasn't so easy. He was more on the stubborn side and might brood a good while. We had to leave him alone for a day or two, whatever it took. It wasn't as easy for him to say "I'm sorry" as it was for Jill.

Our home wasn't that strict overall. They got away with quite a bit, but we wanted them to be good kids and they were always respectful. We never heard them cuss or mouth off in the house. I don't know what they did when they were with their friends – what parent does – but around the house neither of them would act out like that.

Jill and Jeff were close. When they got older, Jeff did his share of teasing his sister, though. He had a way of pushing her buttons – on purpose no doubt. She'd get mad in a minute or less. He had a knack for it. He just knew her, but he loved her even through the torment. When push came to shove, they were there for each other even though they'd pretend otherwise.

Jeff liked Nintendo; he played that a lot. At the time that was the rage, but I never got into it with him. He and I used to watch TV together and we watched just about everything, though he preferred soldier movies and also Star Wars. He was so-so at skateboarding and pretty good at riding his bike. I couldn't wait until he discovered cars!

Jeff also had a go-cart when he was little. Although Janet never wanted him to have one, he pleaded his case well and I decided to buy it. All he could do was drive it around the street, and he couldn't do that much because the police didn't appreciate it. He had to sneak it out! We ended up selling it to a family who lived in the country.

I taught Jeff how to play baseball and basketball. Sometimes he was a little stubborn and didn't want to practice particular techniques so I just let him work through it until he said, "Okay, let's play." Then I could teach him. He liked playing basketball – he liked playing me! He was always trying to gain the upper hand and win, but he couldn't. It was just a friendly rivalry when he was little, but when he got bigger and he *could* win – he thought that was really something!

Jeff, Age 11

Jeff's build was small and thin. He didn't really sprout up until late in high school, and then he grew to six foot! I remember in seventh grade he played on the junior high basketball team. None of the kids were that good, but Jeff was only averaging about forty seconds a game. The coach had a rule that if any of the parents complained about their kids not playing enough, they wouldn't play at all. I didn't like how he was playing Jeff, but the other parents advised me to be quiet about it. After a while I couldn't stand it so I asked the coach why he wasn't playing him more. The coach looked at me levelly and said, "We don't need this conversation."

"Yes, we do," I replied. He gave me some baloney about how the other kids were better. I told him he wasn't a coach to begin with, and he didn't know what he was doing. I left it at that. When a team loses every game by twenty points or more, and some kids are sitting on the bench getting only forty seconds a game, and other kids are playing all the time (especially one whose father is taping the game for the coach), that tends to make the other parents a tad upset. When people don't give kids a chance, that has a long-lasting effect. He instilled in Jeff the belief that he wasn't a good player. He went out for the team for the next two years, but he didn't make it, and Jeff could play. By the time I got done working with him, he could play as well as anyone else. The coach just looked at him and figured because of his size, he couldn't play. When he entered high school he wasn't interested anymore and quit trying, and that's when he started growing, started developing. He could dribble the ball with both hands, and he could shoot. I blame that one coach. If I ever meet him today, I will certainly tell him what I think of his methods.

I might be prejudiced, but I had two great kids. They might have bickered once in a while but I was proud of them. Whenever we socialized they were very polite and never caused any problems. I've seen a lot of kids throwing tantrums in my years, but ours never did. Oh they may have tried when they were young, but we only had to correct them once and that was it. Yes, I was very proud of the way they were growing up.

# 23

# Jill

*(Author's Note: The following are excerpts from Jill's diary, spanning from 1985 at age 12 to 1990, age 17.)*

## February 14, 1985

I gave Brian a valentine and a kiss.

## March 14, 1985

Today is a sad day for Wendy but a happy day for me. Wendy and Brian broke up so now I can have him.

## May 21, 1985

Today Brian confesses he likes me. Shawn says he likes me and I think Kevin does too.

## July 17, 1985

Every day I have been at Brian's. Yesterday our eyes met for the first time. He looked up at me as if to say, "I love you." On the last day of school we had this big shaving cream fight. Brian kept on getting me, is this a good or bad sign?

## November 5, 1985

I have several questions that I can't answer. One, during the summer, Brian was sweet to me and everybody said he liked me. Well ever since school started Brian has been ignoring me. It all started when everybody told him how much I liked him. In the summer we went swimming together. I pitched him baseballs, he pitched me some. I have two ideas why he is ignoring me. #1: I hang around with Wendy and he doesn't like her. #2: He hates my guts. Well where did I go wrong? After all I have liked him for four years.

### *June 13, 1986*

Summer is a peaceful and relaxing time. A time for fun, a time for changing. It's a time for growing and wondering what's up with the boy you like or your best friend. Well that's my idea of summer, or at least part of it. Me and Brian still aren't talking. I feel like such a loser. I tried out for $8^{th}$ grade cheerleading and pom-pons and didn't make it either.

### *July 4, 1986*

Me and Brian still aren't talking. I still think about him a lot. I guess it will take a while to get over him, even though he has a massive body that's so darkly tanned. I feel like such a loser. I mean, if Carolyn and Jenny can make pom-pons, why can't I? Well I guess that's life. Summer is so boring.

### *August 19, 1986*

I'm getting fed up with my brother and my mom. She keeps telling me to treat him nice when he is mean to me. I still like Brian a lot. Every time he passes my house he looks at it, as if expecting to see me, the born loser.

Jill, Age 12

## *May 7, 1987*

I tried out for 9$^{th}$ grade pom-pons. I made it! I love Brian and Mike and Eric.

## *October 29, 1987*

I hate my life. Nobody lets me be me. My parents expect me to be like my straight-A cousins. If I get a C they tell me I'm not trying hard enough. How do they know how hard I'm trying? I'm not perfect. They don't even support me with poms and volleyball. All they say is if I get D's I'm off the pom squad. That's not fair. I told her that, all she said was, "Life's never fair." Sometimes I wish I could just go and hide and cry until I can't cry anymore. I would feel so much better. I wish I could just escape this life and go into a life where I'm always happy.

## *February 17, 1988*

Well quite a bit has happened. I liked Tony but in the back of my mind I liked a boy named Conrad. I don't believe he asked me out but he did. The last two Friday nights me and Christi have been meeting Conrad and a few other people at the skating rink. The second Friday we couple-skated. We were sitting in a booth resting and the whole time he had his arm around me. We sat pretty close. For Valentine's Day the cheerleaders sold balloons. Conrad got me one. It had Mickey's and Minnie's on it and says, "I love you" all over it. I got him the same one. We've been going out for two weeks tomorrow. I don't think I've ever been so happy. I really love Conrad.

## *February 26, 1988*

Hi. I went to the rink again. I had fun until Christi and Joe started bugging me and Conrad about whether or not he's gonna kiss me. Well he did. Twice. The first time was okay but I turned my head. The second time we were couple skating. He went to kiss me again and all I did was look at my skates. I'm so scared. It's the first time I've ever kissed a guy. I feel like such a jerk. After all, we've been going out for three weeks and two days. Help!

## *May 9, 1988*

We've been skating almost every Friday. Last Friday we went skating and guess what? We kissed again. I didn't pull away this time.

I got contacts. That's about it.

## *July 27, 1988*

Guess what. Me and Conrad broke up. I did all the talking. I don't believe it. Five months and two weeks down the drain. He wants to go out with some girl in 7th or 8th grade. Fine with me.

## *January 11, 1990*

Well it's the beginning of a new decade. Quite a bit has happened since I last wrote. I was on the swim team. It was okay. I've been trying to get my knees straightened out, but the doctor says he can't do anything. I'm getting my class ring tomorrow. It's my birthday gift. I got a stereo for Christmas, but it's not as nice as Jeff's TV. They got it from the home shopping club. Well, that's about it.

Love, Jill

# 24

# Janet

1985 was going to be a landmark year for Diane and me. We were both turning forty! As the New Year crept upon us, however, we didn't realize what a drastic turn all our lives would take.

Diane's birthday was first on January 13, and I was close behind on February 19. Actually turning forty wasn't what was bothering me at the time. I was starting to get antsy and felt the urge to branch out. I had always liked being with people and was stagnating after so many years in the home. Diane had a full time career as well as two growing children – she never sat still long enough to get bored! Don't get me wrong, though, I was always happy being a full-time mom. I just started reflecting, thinking maybe I should have done this or that or even went to school. I needed a little more stimulation now that Jeff and Jill were growing up – a little more excitement!

Ideally I would have found a job that fit into our lifestyle and didn't detract from my time with Jill and Jeff, but it didn't work out that way. I ended up working in a bakery, signing on for twenty hours per week. Unfortunately those twenty hours were four days a week from 4:00 to 8:00 PM, then Saturdays 4:00 to 8:00 PM. Not exactly the kind of hours I had been looking for! I had agreed to that schedule because the bakery was always closed on Sundays, so I figured I would at least have one full day of family time. During the week, however, the kids got home at 3:30 PM and I had to leave for work at ten minutes to four! Since Tom worked shift work there was only one week out of four that they were actually home by themselves, and they were certainly old enough by that time anyway. Jill was in junior high. I stuck with the job nevertheless, even though I never liked it. I didn't want to be a quitter! After a couple of years I switched to working for the school system. I was on-call for substitute playground or lunchroom monitor duty. Then I was working the same hours the kids were in school.

Diane and her husband Larry and Tom and I had always stayed close. We would spend Friday or Saturday evening together, and sometimes we would go to church and then out to eat afterwards. Our kids were close too. Diane's daughter Nikki was first, then Jill a couple of years after that, and her son Jason and Jeff were only six weeks apart. Jill and Jeff always referred to Nikki and Jason as their cousins – they always introduced them that way. They were certainly together as much as cousins.

Early in February Larry started to complain of a head cold or what might possibly be an ear infection. One day when Diane was at work, Larry asked their neighbor to take him to the doctor because he couldn't maintain his balance. The doctor prescribed some antibiotics and sent him home. Later that night he fell in his bathroom and couldn't get up. Diane dialed 911 and when the paramedics arrived they figured that since he was so young, only forty-two, he must have hit his head on the wall or the sink. Larry began to drift in and out of consciousness and shortly after he arrived in the ER he became comatose.

Diane didn't call me right away. After a couple of days she had her sister-in-law call us and tell us he had been admitted and was on life support. We were in shock; we really couldn't believe this had happened. From that day on Tom and I were at the hospital every evening after work keeping vigil with Diane.

I remember the first day I went to visit him. As the doors to the elevator opened on his floor, I noticed Diane sitting in a chair directly across. She looked haggard and her eyes were dark with heavy circles. Sitting very still, she raised her head slightly as I walked towards her. Our eyes met and held while she steadily implored, "Now don't cry, Janet, don't cry because you're going to make me cry." I couldn't help but cry. My emotions were hanging on that unsteady precipice between fear and grief. Together we walked into his room. All those horrible machines with their horrid noises! I couldn't even stay calm enough to sit with him for a while. He was so still, but his hands were warm, and he looked so at ease. Why couldn't he just open his eyes? Why must those beepers and hisses from the machines keep sounding? I left his room and never went in again.

His diagnosis was a brain stem aneurysm, and I was there with Diane when the doctor came to explain what that meant. He told her the effects were irreversible. They had already run several brain wave tests and they were all flat. My head was in a whirlwind, and my throat was parched. She would have to make the decision whether to take him off life support or not. With her head hung low and her shoulders slumped, she sobbed. She didn't know what she was going to do without him, she said. He was the light of her life. None of us could fathom life without Larry.

I stayed in the background at the funeral and afterwards because her brother-in-law Andy and his wife stepped up to help Diane. When people step up, I step back. Whenever I felt I was needed, I would go to her. I discovered she was not all that strong. Here was a lady who would get in her car and drive an hour to work in a snowstorm. She was unstoppable, but this was different. This was Larry.

For a long time afterward Diane just went through the motions of living. She was able to follow through with some of the school activities that she and Larry had always done together almost by rote, and when Tom and I went along we noticed how strange it felt not to have Larry with us. His death left a very real void. As time went on she mentioned how she hated being alone and would probably remarry once the kids got old enough to be on their own. I remember how she always wanted a swimming pool in their back yard; that was a constant discussion between her and Larry. After Larry passed away, she never would put that pool in.

Dealing with Larry's death was my first real traumatic experience. It took quite a toll on my nerves by the time everything had settled down again. I had lived through my dad's death, but that was different. He was very sick and was suffering, whereas Larry was a much younger man and healthy by all outward appearances. He had so much to live for. When I think of some of the things we had done together over the years – the four of us... Those were good times, and we were so entwined in each other's lives. We were even godparents for each other's children.

Shortly after Larry's funeral I found out just how hard it had been on my nerves. I experienced my first panic attack. I was sitting in our house with Tom, just talking and relaxing. All of a sudden I felt so dizzy. The doctor said it was probably just anxiety after everything that had happened. I was surprised I didn't have the attack at the time he died, but I was able to function through that. I think it's not until you stop and think, or have the time to reflect, that the panic or fear or whatever it is slaps you down.

In the years following Larry's death I have become even closer to Diane. She knows what it is to lose somebody.

# 25

# Tom

Larry died so young - only forty-two. When you're as close as Larry and I were, it really hurt to lose him. We were buddies. We visited each other's house. We went out to dinner. Our kids played together.

We were also in the army reserves together; we were both medics. I remember one year we had summer camp in Colorado Springs. Everyone urged us, "You've got to drive up Pike's Peak!" So one day we rented a brand new car to do just that. It was an American Motors car – they don't even make those anymore. Larry was driving and we set out to have a great old time. We took off up the mountain but apparently this car didn't have much oomph. There was a tour bus driving in front of us and the driver kept waving Larry around him, so Larry pulled into the other lane – it was only a two-lane road - and just stayed there behind the tour bus! I prodded him, "Why don't you step on it so we can go around them?"

He exclaimed, "What do you think I'm doing? I've got it floored now!" We couldn't get enough power to go any faster. The driver was getting aggravated and finally found a place where he could pull off to let us go by. He was sneering, but of course we were laughing so hard we could barely see through our tears.

Whenever we went to summer camp, we pitched the big hospital tent and then set our little pup tents about fifty yards out from it, forming the perimeter. Although we were supposed to sleep in the pup tents, everybody slept in the big tent. Now the commanders always told us when you set up a hospital, you're never supposed to position it at the bottom of a mountain because of flash floods. So what did they do? Yep - they ordered it placed at the bottom of a mountain. And on the other side of the mountain was the target range for jets! Luckily we had no flash floods that year but during the day the jets would shoot off their rockets for target practice. They would soar right over us and set their afterburners so we got the full effects of their loud bang. They flew so low we could see them laughing!

When it came time to break down the camp, the commanders told us to go out and collect our pup tents. Larry and I looked toward the tents, shook our heads and said, "We're not going out there to get those tents!" Rattlesnakes were sunbathing on the cozy dark green! Those tents could have stayed out there forever as far as we were concerned!

There was a snowstorm in the winter of 1985 when Larry died. He had been complaining of an earache, but we hadn't seen him in a couple of days because of the weather. He went to a nearby doctor who treated him for an ear infection when in fact he was having a stroke. When Diane called for an ambulance that night he was no longer able to stand up, and by the time he arrived at the hospital his speech was slurring, and he quickly fell into a coma.

Although he was in the hospital for several days before he died, he was already brain dead. The doctors said they had to keep him on life support to make sure there was no brain activity, but he was gone - there was no doubt about it. The machines were keeping him what we would *think* of as alive, but he wasn't really alive. I don't believe that.

Every day Diane would go to the hospital and sit. That had to be hard not to be able to talk to him. It was a difficult time for Janet too. When her dad died, he had already been through a long illness, surgery, and he was suffering. With Larry, it was just so quick and unexpected. Who would have thought? It hurt me as badly as it hurt Janet, but I didn't express it the same. Janet actually started having her panic attacks after Larry's funeral.

We explained the situation as best we could to Jill and Jeff. Of course up until the time Larry died, we weren't sure he was going to die. There was always that little hope of a miracle, but eventually the doctors said there was no chance.

Afterwards it seemed like we were even closer to Diane for a time, but then she went her own direction for a while. She needed to regroup. We were always there if she needed us, always did what we could. Later we went on a few vacations together to various resorts. The girls went for spa treatments while I did my best to keep the boys busy. I didn't attempt to be a father figure to Nikki and Jason, but I tried to step in when they needed help. I could never have taken the place of their father; I didn't want to. With situations like that you don't want to intrude too much either. They had their Uncle Andy and his wife and other relatives that were helping, so I did what I could and let events evolve on their own.

I realize the older I get the more I take everything to heart – even thoughts of life and death. Priorities come more into focus, like people and relationships, or maybe I just appreciate them more. When you're young, life gets in the way and sometimes you're too busy to comprehend their importance, but tomorrows are guaranteed to no one.

I remember only good times when I think of Larry. I remember he loved the Three Stooges. I remember how he joked around and cut up. Do I miss him yet today? Sure I do.

# 26

# Janet

Whereas Jill was very outgoing and spirited growing up, Jeff was low-keyed and reserved. I remember when he was in fourth grade he represented his class in the jump-rope contest. He won too, having jumped 506 times, but he did it as a personal challenge just to see how many times he could jump. He only competed against himself.

Jill, on the other hand, relished competition. Things always came harder for her but she kept on trying, whether it was schoolwork, sports, or otherwise. The teen church group is one example. She had fun with it for a while, but then they got a new youth leader who had a tendency to pick and choose the kids. Jill got left out a few times and she was hurt, but she bounced back. She didn't quit – didn't let it get the best of her. I really tried to promote the idea of not quitting. If you sign up for some activity, you stay for the duration. Once you've gone through that, if you don't want to do it again you don't have to. If today's a challenge, tomorrow may be easier.

Jill and Jeff were close, and Jeff managed to express his affection in two very distinct ways. The first was through brotherly teasing, which started when he was about ten-years-old. He loved to rile Jill and would tease her about everything – what she was wearing that day or how her hair was styled – anything to aggravate her. Jill was pretty easy-going but Jeff could push her buttons, and he loved it! Secondly, he gifted her with chicken pox when she was in junior high. Jeff's case was very mild but of course Jill had them top to bottom. She was in misery, and he slid right through.

When Jeff was still fairly young, Diane got me watching the home shopping network and Jeff would sit and watch it with me. Well, that year Jill wanted a stereo for Christmas. I saw one advertised, and of course I didn't know the difference between a good stereo and a mediocre one, so I asked Jeff, "Do you think your sister would like that stereo?"

"Yes, yes, yes!" he answered. So I bought it.

A few years later when he had his own stereo, which was very nice, Jill would comment, "Yeah, look what I got and look what you got." Jeff used to say he never understood why I would ask his opinion when he was so young.

Jill, in fact, always categorized Jeff as a spoiled brat. "Mom lets you do anything you want." "I have to do the dishes and you don't because you're the baby." When we were at the table eating and Jeff wanted ketchup or something I would jump up and get it. "Let him get it himself! You always spoil him!" she would complain. Well I jumped up with her requests too, but she never remembered that.

Both Jeff and Jill had devoted relationships with our entire family, but Jill more so. She had a special connection with my brother Chuck. They were happy just to be together and spent most of their time cutting up. He did say there was one age where she changed, and he didn't like being around her very much. You guessed it – it was puberty. He said she was too irritable; he didn't have a lot of patience with her. No kidding!

Jeff walked in Jill's shadow when it came to family socializing – or socializing of any sort for that matter. He let her be the mouthpiece and he just floated behind. He could be a show-off sometimes, though. I look back on pictures of them growing up and he would forever be goofing off – rather like Tom now that I think about it!

Arnold Swartzeneggar and Sylvester Stallone were Jeff's favorites. In fact, he liked Rambo so much my brother always called him Rambo, or usually "Bo" for short. In grade school, Jeff was in a Christmas play dressed up as a reindeer – antlers and all. For a long time after that my brother called him "Rambo Reindeer." Jeff just laughed it off.

We never had to force Jill or Jeff to do anything. They knew what was expected of them. Especially Jeff, he was never mouthy or a discipline problem. He liked to watch the kung fu and Rambo movies on TV, but I told him, "The words and things you see on TV are not to be used in this house. If I do see or hear them, you will not watch those programs any more." I never did hear him fly off with bad language or abusive behavior, even when he got older.

Whenever Tom and I had a disagreement with Jill, she would sequester herself in her room and write us a long letter, which we usually found on our pillow at bedtime. I saved all those letters purposefully to share with her when she had a child of her own. I knew she would come over one day and say, "Mom, this kid is driving me crazy!" and I would say, "Here Jill, read these." I would want her to know that what she was going through all parents have been through. Here's an example of one:

*"Mom, I don't mean to fight with you but there are things you don't understand, and I know there are things I don't understand. First, let's go to the subject of the car phone. You said it would make you feel more comfortable because I will always have access to a phone. Me and Jeff went looking, but you and Dad didn't have the time. Next, what kid my age doesn't want their own car? Something they are responsible for, something they can call their own. I know I probably can't afford it, but couldn't we at least look? If I look now I'll know what I have to do to save money. I'll have a goal or an idea to aim for. It's not fair that Dad and Jeff call about cars, but the question can't even be discussed with me. There are probably other things, but I can't think of them right now."*

Jill had many friends and always had some puppy-love craze going on. She was the action person and wanted in on everything. She was thrilled to be invited to two Proms, both Junior and Senior. For the Junior Prom she wore a pink and white dress with ruffles. Ruffles were her thing and she loved pink. For her Senior Prom we looked all over for dresses and finally found a very pretty white gown. She loved it but told me, "Oh Mom, this is a little expensive."

"That's okay," I reassured. "I'll just make you wear it for your wedding!" She stood in the mirror wearing that dress and just swayed back and forth looking like a princess.

In high school Jill worked at a shoe store, and one night it was robbed while she was there. The men were even carrying guns, but luckily they just took the money and left. The next day she was too shook up to go to school. We talked about it and even though she was still afraid she decided she would go back to work. I knew she had to go on or else she might keep stepping aside, and eventually she managed to overcome her fear.

When later she told me she was ready to move on to something else, I said that was fine. She started working at the Burger King where her friend worked, and once she had worked there for a while, she was eligible for a program that awarded $1000 a year for college if she continued to work through school. Her boss hurried and got her into that program before they phased it out, so she did receive some help there for college. I had always wanted Jill to work, not for the money, but to teach her to be responsible. Everything I did with my children was for a reason or a lesson. Maybe I tried to teach them too many lessons.

Her high school band was the first local band to play at Disney World. She traveled there on the bus with the school and Tom and Jeff and I drove down a few days earlier. My in-laws were already there so we all got to watch them play at EPCOT. People came up to us afterwards and said what a nice job they had done, and they were right!

It was an awesome experience for everyone when Jill graduated high school in 1991. Our family attended the ceremony and then later we had a big open house at our church hall. It all turned out so nice. Everyone brought in food and baked their special treats, and Jill and Tom decorated the hall with balloons. Jeff was so excited; he was crazy about his big sister. Tom and I presented her with a heart-shaped pendant and chain.

Jill's High School Graduation with her parents

Jill and I would sit and chat at the kitchen table for hours sometimes. We would joke around together – she had a great sense of humor. We went shopping and out to eat like best buddies. One night Tom and Jeff went to a basketball game and even though it was storming, she and I went out to a nice restaurant and made an evening of it. She was my friend, my daughter, my companion. She touched all the bases of my heart.

# 27

# Tom

When Jeff was thirteen years old, he was scheduled to make his First Communion. Janet, Jill, and I were "assigned" the job of writing him a letter expressing how we felt about him and the task before him. Here it is:

"*Jeff*

Thirteen years ago God gave us something very precious. He gave us a son whom we named Jeff. As he grew, so did our love for him.

We understand the CCD program was not something you thought was very important. Jeff, what you have been learning will play a big part in your life. We can already see the love inside of you shine.

When we least expect it you come up with answers about your faith.

Dad and Mom are very proud of you for all your accomplishments, such as A-B Honor Roll and 17-point basketball games. Also, we think about the days when no one would give you a chance to make a basket, so in turn you give others that chance. This is what a good Christian is. Jeff, you have so many good qualities. One of the most important things is to always be yourself and stand by your ability to make good decisions.

Jeff, remember we will always be there for you through all the joys and any problems. You can always count on your family.

Thanks for all the hugs and just sitting and sharing the thoughts of the day.

Love,
Dad, Mom, and Jill"

Rosko Family, 1987

In high school, the tennis coach wanted Jeff to try out for the team so he did, but he was never that good of a player because he didn't practice. The coach, however, had it in his mind he was going to *make* him a good player by teaming him with the opposing team's best player. Jeff would get killed. He didn't get beat all the time, just most of the time! He'd complain, "Look at that, Dad. The coach has me playing against their top player!"

I encouraged, "That's okay, Jeff. You can learn from him." Eventually he got better, but he didn't stick with it long enough to get really good. The coach begged him to come back for another season, but Jeff decided enough was enough.

When Jill started driving, we bought a Camaro from a lady who lived down the street from us. That Camaro was supposed to be a Corvette – for me! We allowed Jill to drive it, however it made me a little nervous because she wasn't the world's greatest driver. Forward she did okay, although her right foot was pretty heavy, but she didn't back up too well. Her mother taught her to drive – she drives the same way. In the winter we'd make her drive the Oldsmobile, and of course Jill didn't appreciate that. We were trying to keep her safe, you see, because the Camaro didn't handle as well when it was icy or wet.

Jeff used to tease Jill about hitting the mailbox when she backed out of the garage even though she had never done that. Well one day she *did* hit the mailbox. He came into the kitchen and proceeded to tease her about it as usual, and this time she really flew off the handle. She thought he already knew about it and was teasing her anyway, but of course he hadn't known. When he found out, he *really* got on her and choked up laughing so hard. She stomped upstairs crying. I thought it was all pretty funny, which of course didn't make the situation any better. She came by her driving skills honestly, though. I had a steel toolbox with a lock on it sitting in the garage. One day Janet pulled in and hit the lock, breaking it off the toolbox. She didn't even touch the toolbox. It wasn't dented – there wasn't a mark on it. How she could do that without touching the box I don't know. Didn't hurt the car, either. Heck, that's good driving.

Jill scraped the car when she hit the mailbox, though. She was afraid, thinking I was going to yell at her, which of course I did. I didn't want to disappoint her. Afterwards Jeff suggested, "Gee, Dad, we need to put the mailbox on the right side of the driveway so we can get the other side of the car fixed." The insurance had put a whole new left side on so Jeff thought we should work on the right side next.

She had a couple of episodes with the car, actually. When she was working at Burger King, she pulled out in front of another car and smashed the front end. I put the car in the shop, and the very same day we got it out, she took the car to school and a guy hit her in the fender. I really got mad that time! She was scared and crying, but I settled her down. It wasn't her fault. It's just that we had gone through all the aggravation of getting the car fixed and now we had to go through it all over again. That's part of life, I guess, and at least she hadn't gotten hurt.

Even though Jeff loved to tease Jill and get her riled, they had a good relationship with each other. They had their little spits and spats. Sometimes he would get mad at her, sometimes she would tell on him. But if Jeff got mad, he would say something and it would be over. If Jill got mad, she would storm upstairs and slam the door. However, if one got their feelings hurt and was crying (of course you never saw Jeff cry much), the other would mellow out and try to help. They loved and supported each other when it came down to it.

Jill started dating when she was fifteen or sixteen. I didn't have any father-daughter talks with her beforehand; I left that up to her mother. I checked the boys out, though, and gave them a little talk. I told them to have her home on time, no drinking, and keep their hands to themselves if they wanted them back - just general stuff like that.

Every year Jill would faithfully try out for cheerleading, but she never made it, though she did belong to pom pons because it was a larger group. She was a swimmer too and swam the last two years of high school. The first year she did okay. The girls on her team were better swimmers, and since she had to keep up with them, she became better herself. She learned to be more competitive and she grew from that. I had to give her a lot of credit with her swimming. She had floating kneecaps which were very painful for her; she even had to wear a rubber knee protector to help keep the kneecaps in place. It caused cramping in her calves, mostly in the middle of the night. She would wake up crying in pain and call me to massage her legs and do what I could. We tried everything – ice, heat, aspirin, etc. She was putting so much tension on those knees, but she wouldn't stop swimming. We couldn't make her stop. She had that kind of determination. She wouldn't score first or second – maybe fifth or sixth – but she did well for her limited ability. It just made her try harder.

Jill certainly had a temper. She was good overall but there were those times when you got her mad... I remember one time, she was probably sixteen or seventeen, we got into it and she stormed up to her room. Janet's brother Chuck came over shortly afterwards and asked, "Where's Sissy?" (He always called her Sissy.)

I said, "Well, she's upstairs. She's a little mad."

He was confident and reassured, "Oh, I'll go up there and smooth her down."

"Chuck," I warned him, "if I were you I wouldn't go up those stairs."

"That's okay," he said, "She'll let Uncle Chuckie in her room." So he went upstairs and I heard him walk across the hall and knock on her door.

"Get out of here!" she yelled.

He ran down those stairs so fast, and of course I had to say, "I told you so." When she was mad, she just wanted to be alone.

Once she started to calm down, she would always write us letters.

Here's one:

*"Mom and Dad, we need to talk. I'm writing this down because if I don't I might get sarcastic. I'm now seventeen and almost a senior in high school...I will always love you guys more than anyone or anything else. But it's time I start to grow up. It should be up to me when I want to be with my friends. You need to loosen the reins. I'm almost an adult.*

*Do you realize that next year I can vote? It's time to face the fact that 'Little Jilly' has grown up! The day I get married (it won't be for a while) you guys are going to be a mess. It's time I start learning from my own mistakes... So please think about what I've said.*

*Love always,<br>Jill"*

She was never really a discipline problem, though. Some things just made her angry, like if we wouldn't let her have the car or stay out late. She would argue, "But the other kids can do it!" You know the routine. All kids are like that - you were probably like that and so was I. That's just the experience of growing up.

# 28

# Janet

In 1990, when I was still working at the bakery, one of my friends told me about a job opening with the Town of Merrillville. Supposedly, one department had a position available and was having a hard time finding anyone to fill it. So I went there one day in February, walked in and inquired about the job, and they asked, "Do you smoke?"

I replied, "No."

They said, "You're hired!" There were no other applicants; it was as simple as that.

Later, my boss joked, "If I knew you were left-handed I would never have hired you."

I started as a clerk and did filing, then moved on to doing building permits and licensing contractors. We all had many jobs in the office and eventually as more people were hired, I was promoted up through the ranks, so it wasn't a dead-end position. It was also convenient to home and close to the school, and in fact the kids dropped in frequently and everyone got to know them pretty well. It was a real family atmosphere – your home life always came first. If you had to leave to take care of a sick child or quit early to get to a school game, no questions were asked.

My job enabled me to work with people, too, which is something I enjoy. There are a lot of nice people out there, a lot of interesting people, and you develop friendships even though you only see them once a month or so. You start asking about their kids or how their mom's doing – you learn what their likes and dislikes are. Sometimes they can be contrary and demanding, but overall, it's rewarding. I would never want to give up my job. It's part of my therapy for living.

*No Words*

When Jeff turned sixteen, I suggested he go job-hunting at the Ross Township Parks Department. Many of the area kids went there to work, and it was a good experience for them mowing lawns and keeping the ball fields ready for games. Jeff enjoyed it, although I think he got in trouble a few times. Once at the end of the season he came home and proclaimed, "Guess what Mom, I got fired today."

My shoulders slumped and I chastised, "Oh Jeffrey, what do you mean you got fired?" He proceeded to tell me that that day all the kids went to lunch together and brought it back to the job to eat. They got caught in traffic on the way back and were late, so the boss told them their lunch hour was over and they had to get to work. All the other kids threw their lunches away, but Jeff wasn't about to. He said he paid for his lunch and was going to eat it, not toss it in the trash. He laughed and told me not to worry because at the end of the day the boss hired him back. He liked to perturb people sometimes for fun, but they liked him anyway.

Jeff never helped out around the house too much, though. He hated to mow the lawn. Jill mowed the lawn and so did Tom and I, but not Jeff. He didn't do too much of anything, come to think of it, only if you really begged him. Jeff liked to tinker, though - liked to work with his hands. If Tom were building a deck or something, Jeff would be right there to help him.

Jeff didn't seem to have many friends calling him – girls or boys. I wondered about that because I thought he was so good looking, yet there were no girls calling. Once in a while we would go to the mall together, however, and we couldn't leave without two or three girls greeting, "Hi Jeff, how are you?" He would just smile and walk on.

Jeff had the ability to make good grades but he would wait till the end of the grading period, sloughing off for the first half and carefully calculating the point where he would have to kick it in gear. Then he did. He knew exactly how much he had to do to pull a "B." It wasn't his style to carry an even pace throughout.

The older Jeff and Jill got, the closer they became. They started doing more together, like going shopping or out driving.

One day in 1993 they went dog shopping, deciding it was time to replace our dog that had passed away. They drove to the animal shelter and picked out Mandy. I had to sign for her, though, so they came to my work and said, "Oh Mom, we found this really cute dog. Can you go with us to get her?" Well how can you say no to your kids? Besides, she was *very* cute – yellow and fluffy, calm and quiet. Tom came home from work that night and sat on the floor in the kitchen to play with her. The puppy didn't even come near him! She was afraid of everybody except Jeff and Jill. Eventually she grew into us, though, and now she thinks she's one of us.

Jill had decided early on that she wanted to become a nurse. She must have known when she was very little because a couple of times she even dressed as a nurse for Halloween. She was also interested in paramedics and actually took a course and was registered shortly after high school. Her idea was to work part-time as a paramedic and go to nursing school too.

She put in several college applications and was accepted at Valparaiso University, Indiana University, and Purdue, and of those she chose Purdue. Purdue Calumet campus was within driving distance of our home so she could still live with us. We had told her she could go to the main campus in Lafayette, but we never pushed it. I don't think she was ready to leave home.

She never worked as a paramedic. Those jobs were hard to come by, and paramedics might have to work three different services at one time to get in a full week. When she started nursing school the professors acted like they weren't thrilled for her to have that training, anyway. Besides, she went to college full time and that was enough work as it was. She still kept her job at Burger King, which was a mistake on my part. I had already decided that when Jeff was ready for college, I wasn't going to let him work and go to school too.

Jill liked being in college. She was always excited about what she was learning or what activities were going on. She would come home tired and dragging sometimes or bummed out because the day didn't go like she had anticipated, but she took everything in stride. She developed some strong friendships while she was there too.

She never had second thoughts about the nursing profession. Maybe her interest initially formed through my sister Betty, hearing her nursing stories as she was growing up, or perhaps even through Tom and his stories about being a medic in the army. She liked trauma care and intended to specialize in that area. She wanted to work in an emergency department or on the Lifeline helicopter units, whichever offered the most excitement! She even packed a little bag of medical supplies and kept it in her car, just in case she happened on an accident.

After attending Purdue for two years, she and a few other students were having trouble getting the classes they needed. The courses filled up quickly and Jill was forced to take some other courses that she really didn't need. Along with a couple of older students, Jill made the decision to transfer to Valparaiso University in her junior year. Although Valparaiso was a little farther away from home, it was still close enough that she could commute.

Her advisor at VU frequently requested she come see her about her grades or her progress in general. Jill struggled for her grades at Purdue, and VU was even tougher. One day I jokingly said to Jill, "You know, you go in there so often you really should start taking her coffee and donuts. Kill her with kindness." We always laughed about that.

Overall she managed fine and liked her clinical courses particularly well. In her diary she wrote about the neonatal unit being so much different than she expected. She said the babies didn't "do anything," and she just sat and watched them. After the neonatal experience she did her psychiatric rotation at a hospital in Michigan City. I didn't want her going to Michigan City; it was too far away. I asked her if she could change to a closer hospital, but she told me that would mean upsetting the track she was on. After Michigan City she was scheduled for a hospital in Crown Point which would be closer to home. All we had to do was make it through Michigan City.

On her twenty-first birthday she partied with some friends from school. She stayed out very late and of course I was always worried something was going to happen. She knew I was angry when she got home and the next morning Jeff said I was wrong to have reacted that way. "Mother, you shouldn't have yelled at her because she was out having a good time. It was her birthday, after all, and she had every right." He was holding up for her. I was always hovering, though. Hard to see them grow up, I suppose.

Jill always looked forward to getting married and having a family. I encouraged her to go through school and get her degree first, which she never doubted she would, and then maybe take some trips and enjoy herself after she had worked so hard, but I knew the decision was entirely up to her. I would be happy when she found someone she loved and wanted to marry, whenever that was. We talked about picking out wedding dresses too; she liked the frilly, full dresses with lots of lace. Then the subject of grandchildren would always come up, and I just knew I would make the best grandma. She told me the man she was dating at the time wanted a large family. I was secretly overjoyed and reassured her, "Well, Jill, I'm sure we can deal with that."

# 29

# Tom

Jeff was a good driver - definitely more cautious than Jill. The faster Jill talked, the faster she drove. Her Uncle Chuck used to say whenever he rode with her he would remind her, "Sissy, slow this car down." I believe I taught them both to drive, though. Come to think of it, maybe Janet taught them because she was a better driver than I was. Anybody who could knock a lock off a toolbox without scratching the toolbox had to be great.

Jeff always wanted a '67 Mustang Fastback. He went on and on about it and eventually I got tired of listening to him and said, "Okay, Jeff, if you can find one that's in decent shape I'll go in with you and we'll buy it." He started looking in the paper, car magazines, every place he could think of. He finally spotted one in the paper for $1000. I warned him, "Jeff, stop and think - a $1000 car? It's either in five hundred pieces or it's completely rusted."

He pleaded, "Oh Dad, we've got to go look at it anyway."

"Okay, we can do that," I promised. So we went to see it, and the lady told us it was in the backyard. There it sat. It was completely stripped down. The rear axles, the dashboard - everything was on the seats. It was all rusted. It's like the guy gave up on it. I couldn't help from laughing, but I knew it broke Jeff's heart. I said, "Well Jeff, I told you it was either going to be in five hundred pieces or all rusted, and it looks like it's both."

One day Janet, Jeff, and I were driving to my parent's house and we passed a car dealership. A white '92 Mustang was sitting in the lot. Pointing it out, I said, "Look Jeff, that's a nice-looking car."

He shook his head. "I want a '67." So we went on to my mom and dad's, and on the way back I asked if he wanted to stop and see it. He agreed, and he really liked it. We made them an offer and following a few days of bickering, we finally got the price we wanted. After he'd had it for a while, he confided, "Dad, I really love my car. I'm sure glad I got this one instead of a '67." He loved it! He took care of that car too – kept it clean and even put some money into it. He was a hot rod, though. He didn't buy a five-speed 5.0 for no reason!

It was most definitely important to me that both Jill and Jeff got a college education. Kids today have a hard enough time even with a college degree and those without it, unless they have a trade or something like that, have a difficult time surviving.

Jeff, Age 16, and Jill, Age 20, Last Photo Together

All during high school we encouraged them towards college. We always pushed them to get their homework done and get good grades because that was going to be important. They had to know how to study and how to take tests. I didn't want them to be like me, you see. The steel mill was fine for me, but not for them. We always wanted better for our kids - I think everybody does.

Luckily, Jill and Jeff knew what they wanted to do with their lives well ahead of time. I think Jill decided she wanted to be a nurse as early as junior high. The idea of nursing was something she just came to love, and that was fine with me. They needed to choose their own path because they were going to be on that path for the rest of their lives. I never wanted them to come back and say, "Well, you wanted me to do this, I didn't." "No," I would have emphasized. "*You* wanted to do this."

She decided on Purdue Calumet but started running into problems there because of the system they had for taking classes. The students weren't allowed to officially start in the nursing program till after their freshman year, and then they had to make an application to the program. If they weren't accepted, which she wasn't, they had to wait until the next year to re-apply. It threw off her whole schedule and would have actually taken five or six years to complete a four-year program. We couldn't see that happening.

She then decided to transfer to Valparaiso University, which we all felt was a good move. She was automatically accepted into the nursing program there so she could complete her last two years without any interruption. At that point she was finally working toward the degree she wanted.

Remember nothing came easy for Jill, and her college courses gave her some problems. Anatomy and Physiology really tripped her up and in fact she had to repeat that course. I hated to see her get bad grades but certain courses are just harder for certain people. I was just happy she wasn't going to quit. With Jill, it wasn't a matter of *if* she was going to get it, it was a matter of *when*. She was determined to be a nurse and that was that.

Once she started her clinical courses at VU she really got excited. She enjoyed helping people so much. We would chat a little about medical things, her and I, with my experience as a medic, even though by that time she had a lot more training than I ever had. I would know what she was referring to at least, and I never tried to give her advice!

She was putting in a lot of hours at school and working too. I'm sure her load was frustrating for her at times. We all decided that in her senior year she would live on campus, quitting her job and experiencing campus life. She was really looking forward to that, and I was happy she was going to get that chance. That chance never came around.

# 30

# Tom and Janet

*(Author's note: Tom's words are in italics and Janet's are in regular script.)*

*There are tragedies in life that are so profound that nothing is the same afterwards – and we never see them coming. This one came like a thief and robbed not only our happiness, but the hopes we had so carefully carved for the future.*

There was nothing extraordinary about that Wednesday in February. Life was usual. That morning I was getting ready to go to work and Jeff was going off to school. Jill was leaving for one of her nursing classes and Tom was still sleeping because he had to work the afternoon shift.

Jill was in her second semester of her junior year at Valparaiso University. Every Wednesday she would leave for school early in the morning, attend classes all day, and then spend the night at my sister Betty's house. Her hospital rotation on Thursday was very early, and Betty lived much closer to campus than we did. It was more convenient for her to stay there.

That particular Wednesday morning, February 23, the snow had already begun to fall. I remember talking to Jill about the weather and the road conditions, and she was debating if she should chance the drive to school. Those constant fears of mine rose to the surface yet again, but I didn't want their crippling effect to spill over on Jill. I encouraged her to make up her own mind, telling her, "If you think you can make it then go, and if not turn around and come home." She decided to try it. As she got closer to Valparaiso, the snow kept getting deeper and then the only plausible decision was to keep going. Follow the traffic. Eventually she called me at work to say she had made it, although a little late. She was fine, and I pushed those old fears back down again.

After classes she went on to Betty's house to spend the night as usual. I called my sister that evening to check the weather conditions and she offered to put Jill on the phone. I told her, "No, if she's doing school work don't bother her." She insisted, and Jill got on the line.

"Hi Mom, everything's fine. I'll see you tomorrow. Love you." That was the last time I talked to her.

Jill got up Thursday morning and had breakfast with her cousin Susan. She tried backing the car out of the driveway and got stuck, but her Uncle Bob was able to push her out. Betty told me she was always waiting for the day when the weather would be so bad that Bob would just tell Jill she couldn't go to school. She thought for sure that would be the day, but by then the heaviest snow had fallen the day before and had already begun to melt.

*Jill drove to the university to meet four other girls. The five of them carpooled to the hospital in Michigan City, which was some distance away. That day they were all completing their psychiatric rotation. It was the last time they would have to make the trip to Michigan City. It was her friend Adrienne's turn to drive.*

*By 11:00 AM they had completed their clinical and were headed back to campus. The road conditions were fairly clear by that time, but on Highway 421 there's a low-lying area that has been known to get slick.*

My cousin lives right in that area and about noon his kids were headed home. They called him from their car phone and said there had been a very severe accident and traffic was all backed up. They were safe, but they'd be home a little late.

Around 3:00 PM I was sitting at my desk in the Town Hall, and as I glanced up I noticed the Assistant Chief of Police walk by. He seemed a little nervous and his skin was pale, but the fact that he barely made eye contact with me as he said, "I'm looking for your boss, Janet," is what tightened my heart.

I reasoned with myself, "Janet, don't buy trouble. Leave it be."

Then my boss appeared at my desk, and my breath caught in my throat. "Jill's been in a serious accident and we need to call Tom right away. Can you give me his number?" Yes I could, I thought, but pulling air into my lungs was like pulling cotton through a sieve. "Give me the number, give me the number," she kept imploring.

"I'm giving it to you!" was all I could answer back. After I found it, I was shuffled into a back office as shock and disbelief were spreading through me like wildfire. Someone had called our priest, Father Jerry, and when he walked in the room, I knew Jill was dead.

*About that time I was in the locker room at work getting ready to start my shift. Somebody came and got me, saying I had an important phone call. I went to answer it in my boss's office, and it was Janet's boss, Mabel. "Tom, you need to come and comfort Janet."*

*The hairs on the back of my neck began to prickle and I asked, "Why, what's wrong?"*

*"There's been an accident and Jill got hurt," she told me.*

*My stomach tightened like it was in a vise but somehow I got out the words, "Did she get killed?"*

*"Come comfort Janet, Tom." By what she wouldn't tell me, I knew she was dead.*

*My mind was in a stagnant whirlwind as I drove to Janet's office. Agonizing questions hammered at me but festered with no immediate answers. How? Why? When I finally arrived a blur of people with strained faces took me to Janet. Her eyes and cheeks were wet and red and her body appeared rigid as though it were wrapped in steel. Father Jerry sat close to her and mirrored the same strained look that all the other people had. They both started talking at the same time, telling me we had lost Jill, but I had already known in my heart she was gone.*

Somehow I had managed to have the where-with-all to call my brother-in-law Jerry and my sister Betty before Tom arrived. Even in such emotional torment my mind was clicking with details of what had to be done. Perhaps it was a release of one small part of me to carry on while the rest of me still staggered in disbelief.

Why I did not leave to go home immediately after getting the news instead of being held captive waiting for Tom, I don't know. It is something I regret to the core of my soul. As it was, Tom and I drove home together. When we walked in, Jeff was coming down the stairs from his bedroom. His eyes were glazed and swollen and his arms were limp by his side. My brother Chuck had called the house before we arrived, and I guess he thought enough time had passed since the accident that Jeff would have known about it. He asked, "Jeff, what are you doing?"

Jeff answered, "I'm waiting for Jill to come home. We're going shopping."

Chuck just said, "But Jeff, Jill's dead." That's how he found out. I suppose Chuck felt that he was reinforcing what he already knew and just couldn't accept, but he didn't know and my heart agonized that I hadn't been there for him. He was all alone!

Jeff looked at Tom and me and said in a throaty whisper, "Uncle Chuck called."

*The phone started ringing non-stop and remained a constant background noise throughout the evening. Our brothers and sisters, their husbands and wives, and Janet's mom all began to filter into our home and our consciousness. Janet and I were going through motions. Our actions, our conversation, and our emotions drained our energies to the point of numbed wakefulness. There was still a haze of disbelief piercing us. We were trying to make heads or tails out of what was happening, but we just couldn't do it.*

It just wasn't real to us. We walked from room to room and all those people were there, but Jill wasn't. Your rational mind tells you, "Well, she's probably at school or with her friends." It's the irrational mind that says, "No, Jill's dead."

It helped to a certain degree to have so many people around that first day. There was good and bad in it. People wanted to be there and help us and that kept us from sitting there alone wrapped in tormenting sorrow. We didn't have time to dwell on our devastation, and maybe that's why they stayed close, but on the other hand we didn't have any private time either, and we were so very tired. You know how it feels to be so tired? It hurts to breathe and blink and swallow. It hurts to think, and it hurts not to think.

It would have been calming if Tom, Jeff, and I could have sat together quietly to talk or to cry. We never had that, and after that evening Jeff never talked much about losing Jill. He kept his feelings wrapped inside.

*I don't even know who told us about the actual accident. You would think I would be in the front line demanding details, but it wasn't like that. The fact that Jill had died threw everything else out of focus. Eventually I think Betty talked to the police and in the days following there were several articles in our newspapers. Apparently there were five girls in the car and Jill was sitting in the middle of the back seat. They were driving south down the county highway and a van was driving north. For some reason the driver Adrienne lost control of the car. Whether they were joking around, going too fast, or sliding on ice we don't know. Their car crossed the yellow line and went off in a ditch. We were later told that Julie, who was riding in the front passenger seat, said at that time she felt very lucky because they were stopped and okay. Then the van rammed into the back of the car, peeling off the roof like a can opener. The Nissan Sentra they were driving looked like a pick-up truck when it was over. The three girls in the back seat* were thrown out of the car and died instantly. Kim Pressel and Laura Van Dyke were their names, along with Jill. Adrienne ended up with neck and back injuries and was admitted to the hospital in serious condition. She had been knocked unconscious by the accident but awoke and started screaming when the paramedics arrived. Julie had a broken rib and other injuries but was listed in good condition. The fifty-two-year-old man driving the van wasn't hurt, but very upset, which he should have been. I saw a picture of the car a time later and I couldn't help wondering why he couldn't have gone the other way instead of towards the car. I don't know, maybe he was sliding too. I couldn't understand how the van could have hit so hard to do all that damage.

The newspaper stated that another nursing student, who was also headed back to campus, was the first to arrive at the scene of the accident. She didn't even know the girls' identities until she went up to one of the bodies to check for vital signs and noticed a student-nurse nametag. That young woman drove all the way back to campus and told the professors what had happened. Two of the professors immediately went to the hospital where the two surviving girls were taken to be with them until their families arrived.

We're not sure who identified Jill, but the paper reported that other students did. We also learned later from the police that no one was ticketed because it was just an accident. No one caused it, no one did anything wrong.

"No one was to blame. It was just an accident." What do those words mean? Jill was gone forever. Eventually everyone started going home that Thursday night, home to their own families. But Jill wasn't coming home. The three of us fell exhausted into our beds, but Jill wasn't going to bed. Everyone was saying how sorry they were, how much they would miss Jill. But Jill was young and vibrant. She was working so hard to achieve her goals and had her whole life in front of her. She was compassionate, sincere, and full of love and light. The world would be a better place with her than without her. "We're so sorry, Janet." I'm so sorry! Why is Jill not here? Why was she taken? What will our lives be without her?

# 31

# Tom and Janet

*(Author's note: Tom's words are in italics and Janet's are in regular script.)*

*I don't know how much sleep we got that night. I think the three of us lay mostly in that unsettled state between wakefulness and rest. I know I awoke feeling as though I had done battle with a hated enemy. The shock and disbelief I felt on the first day was being nudged out by absolute grief and devastation. Maybe it's called after-shock, I don't know. I was more able to think about events, and I was certainly more emotional than the first day. I knew there were things that had to be done now for Jill, and I was set upon accomplishing them.*

For me, the shock was not yet subsiding on the second day. What I felt most was emptiness. There was a hollowness in my heart that used to be filled with love and warmth. People started coming to the house again saying how sorry they were, and I was answering, "Thank you" like a recorder set on rewind. When someone hugged me or I hugged them, I felt no comfort. The void was just overwhelming.

Father Jerry arrived early, saying when he woke up that morning he was thinking it was all a terrible dream. He grasped with a finality that it wasn't, and the verity stuck in his throat like a wooden peg.

Jeff had decided he would go to school as usual. I deduced that was his way of dealing with the situation and can remember wondering if his classmates would think it strange for him to be in school the day after his sister's death, but to me that took a lot of courage. Like the rest of us, Jeff was finding the strength to do what he felt had to be done.

*I watched Janet constantly. I didn't know what to expect, you know? I tried to help, tried to keep her from becoming too emotional. We had to concentrate on the tasks at hand, and if she crumbled I would have followed close behind. So we gave each other support, and anything she needed I tried to assist her with. Her movements were so slow, as though she had to will each action. Her face was drawn and hollow.*

*There still was not much time to be alone and talk. We would sit at the kitchen table, but then someone would come in or pull us in a different direction or the phone would ring. At least I was there if she needed me. We had always looked out for each other anyway. It was just so important to me that she was managing to endure.*

I kept my eye on Tom. I watched to see where he was and what his emotions were. He was solemn, calm, and attentive. He was my strongest guidepost, however there were others too. My sister and Diane were there for us as well, especially for the routine activities. "Come on, let's eat now." "Time to get ready to go now."

The Rendina family went to our church and owned a funeral home so it was natural for us to call them. We felt comfortable with them. That morning they went to retrieve Jill's body, and we went to the funeral home that afternoon to begin making the arrangements. My brother's wife, Joene, and Betty went with us.

Everything had to be special for Jill. You know how you help your daughter look special for Prom or help her plan a celebration of some sort, and you want everything to be perfect – just for her? It's because she's your daughter and you love her with all your heart. You work hard to make it special because she's special to you. This was the last thing we could do for Jill. Even though my head was hurting and my eyes were swollen from crying, it had to be special, and I just had to think of the details.

*The Rendina's had known Jill and did everything possible to help us through this time. When we met with them that afternoon, they told us they thought it would be better if we didn't see Jill. They recommended a closed casket. She had died of head injuries and although they were willing to do whatever it took to make her as presentable as possible, it wouldn't do her justice. I wanted to see Jill, or at least see the pictures they had taken of her, but they wouldn't let me. They were our friends, and they thought it would be too hard. So we never got to see her; we never got to say goodbye.*

It was almost unbearable to hear him tell us we couldn't see our beautiful Jill. That hollowness inside me began overflowing with pain once more, but I knew I wouldn't have wanted to see her mangled image every time I closed my eyes. With Betty and Joene's help, we forcibly turned our considerations to the other arrangements. Jill loved pink and I had once seen a rose-colored casket. Even though they didn't have one like that, they were able to locate one for us. The night before I had gone through Jill's closet and picked out one of her favorite dresses and my mother had given me a pair of crocheted slippers that a friend of hers had made.

*Jill had a teddy bear that was special to her, and we fought with the idea of whether or not to put it in the casket with her. In a way we wanted to keep it, but we mentioned it to Jeff and he said, "No, she should have it. That bear went everywhere with her." So that went in the casket too.*

We made sure that Jeff was included in all the arrangements we made for Jill. If there was something he wanted, it was, "Fine Jeff, if that's how you feel." He went along with us to pick out the gravesite too. At the time we only purchased three gravesites, but when everything was over we could see that Jeff felt bad about that. Eventually, we went back and bought the other three so that we had the whole block, never thinking we would ever need it, but it made Jeff feel more at ease.

The flowers we picked out were pink and purple, more of Jill's favorites.

*I remember it snowed real hard that day too. Everyone said, "Oh, Jill's around." It was snowing just like it always did on her birthday in January. We always had blizzards on her birthday.*

We even picked out music that Jill would have liked including some of those she had sung in the church choir. We also scheduled a soloist to sing *A Whole New World* from *Aladdin*, and *Memories*. Our neighbor from across the street later mentioned that the music was very touching. She said it had Jill's "flow" to it.

*Friday and Saturday were hectic days. Family had begun arriving from out of town. My brother Don came in from Oklahoma and my parents arrived from Florida. People were still congregating at our house and the phone kept on ringing.*

Luckily the neighbors and our friends had carried in large amounts of food, more than we could possibly eat. With Tom's parents and my mom having out of town guests, I split up the trays to all the households. Even through my feelings of desperation and emptiness, the kindness of people overwhelmed me. People that you didn't imagine would stop by, did. Neighbors at the end of the block that we just waved to every day as we drove home from work brought food. We had new neighbors across the street that we hadn't known very long at all – they came over and brought something. People I knew from the office that I only dealt with once a week or so – you didn't expect them to get so involved, but they did. I was amazed at how much of the community came to our support.

*Even the funeral home protected us from as much hardship as possible. They ended up paying for everything and told us when we felt up to it, we could come in and settle up. They didn't even say, "Come back in two weeks and pay your bill." They just said take your time and when you're feeling up to it, come in.*

There was nothing done for us that we didn't appreciate. Even though the three of us could have used more time alone with each other and our thoughts, we knew that all our family and friends had nothing but our best interests at heart. People genuinely shared in our tragedy.

*Sunday was the wake and by that time our exhaustion was being replaced by a dazed void. Emotionally we were in a world of our own. Visitation was from 2:00 to 8:00 PM, so we knew it was going to be a long day.*

I had spent much more time picking out Jill's clothing than I had my own and ended up just pulling something out of my closet. They had told me to wear flat shoes, though, and I'm glad I did. We had a continuous flow of people; there was no sitting down. It was as though I was sitting along a highway watching cars go by. That's how people were coming through there, all so quickly and saying the same thing.

*We talked to so many people I couldn't tell you who was there and who wasn't. I can pick out certain people in my mind, although I don't know why. The Dean of Nursing was there and so was the President of Valparaiso University and his wife. I was just standing beside Janet greeting everyone. Jeff stayed in the background with his cousins.*

Jill's boyfriend came through the door with his brother. He was an emotional person and that day he was almost hysterical. The closer he got to us in the long line of people, the worse he became. Finally, Tom told his brother that he should take him out for his own best interests, so that's what he did.

One of Jill's grade school teachers came and brought an angel pin for Jill. I think she was surprised to see the closed casket, but we gave the pin to Mr. Rendina and I'm sure he put it on for us later.

*We were standing there for what seemed to be hours and finally someone said it was time to go sit down for a while and eat something. I know I was glad for that break, especially for Janet's sake. I just don't remember much more. I remember being there and talking to people but not many details. We understood what was happening but our grief was all-consuming. It was like having a mental breakdown.*

One thing I do remember is Tom's dad. Every time someone put a fingerprint or a smudge on the casket he would go up there and polish it with his sleeve. I agonized, "Oh Grandpa, Grandpa, polishing that pretty pink casket." Everyone who loved Jill was overcome by grief and despair.

*Much of my despair came from having a closed casket. It tore me to have to talk to and touch a box rather than my daughter, but it might have been worse having it open and seeing her there with us, lifeless and broken. Yet I would have given anything for that final goodbye.*

The funeral mass was Monday morning at St. Stephen's Church. We arrived first at the funeral home and said prayers. Everyone filed by her casket, and finally we were alone with her and our immediate family.

*It would be difficult for anyone to imagine our desperation at that moment. The thought of having her taken away aroused a low level panic. She would be severed from us, from me. I couldn't be there for her anymore. I couldn't take care of her. It was one of the hardest moments I had to endure up to that point, and there had already been so much suffering.*

*It hit Jeff hard too. I don't remember him expressing much emotion until the day of the funeral itself. He was seventeen-years-old and a junior in high school, just like I was seventeen when my brother Butch died. It really didn't hit me until the funeral either.*

The funeral at St. Stephen's was a very nice service with two priests officiating as well as two deacons. After the mass we traveled to the cemetery and because of inclement weather we had the service indoors at the mausoleum rather than at the gravesite. Her paramedic friends drove their emergency vehicles with their lights flashing in the procession.

*There were so many people; the cars just kept coming through the cemetery gates. The service was short, and everyone took a final pass by the casket. We were alone with her for the last time, but by then we were so exhausted it was hard to feel anymore. The Rendina's stayed with her until she was laid to rest, and the funeral car drove everyone by the gravesite on the way out so they would know where it was located.*

Afterwards we had a catered dinner at our church. Then we came home with just a few family members while others went back to the funeral home to pick up the remaining flowers and bring them back to our house. We had flowers everywhere.

We later arranged for her headstone. They had just begun the process of etching on headstones. To me, angels and water and butterflies are very peaceful. We ordered an etching of an angel looking down into a little stream with some rocks and butterflies all around. Jeff spoke up and said he wanted praying hands in one corner – this from the guy who never wanted to go to church. There's a rosary and cross on it too. We had Mickey Mouse and the medical insignia engraved on her footstone. Everything was Jill, everything was special.

*And everyone who was there for us was special. We appreciated that they stuck by us and helped with the decisions and guided us through those painful hours and days. At the same time Janet and I had to watch out for them as well, especially our parents because of their ages. We were parenting our family, of a sort. We weren't thinking about ourselves much.*

We were so overwhelmed by Jill's loss. Everything that anyone did was out of the love they had for our family and for Jill. It was out of concern and graciousness and sincerity. There was no negativity at all.

*We just made it through those days. Other people were there showing us the way. It wasn't so much in what they said, because what can you say? No words could have lessened our grief, no words would give back our Jill.*

All that mattered was that Jill was so loved and people thought so much of her that they came out. For whatever reason, they came.

# 32

# Janet

I wholly regret during those first few hectic days after Jill's death I did not make time to sit and talk with Jeff about her loss. There was such a blur of activity and in the scarce quiet moments I had, I was utterly exhausted. I watched Jeff and knew our families were looking after him as well, and he was quiet as usual and seemed to just go along with the program. The only time I even noticed his eyes were red was the day of the accident after he first learned the news. I simply thought I would have a better opportunity to talk to him after the funeral when the immediacy of the situation was calming. There's where you always look for tomorrow, but you really have to deal with important things today. There might not be a tomorrow. That's how it was with my mom.

My mom had been at our house along with the rest of the family during the days after Jill's death. She sat in an easy chair and visited with the out-of-town relatives, and I watched her from across the room to make sure she was alright. Jill and my mom were close – she had been the first granddaughter. I was actually looking forward to talking to my mom about Jill's loss; I felt she was the one person who would understand most what I was feeling. She would comprehend the emptiness.

After the funeral dinner we all came back to our house. My mom was talking to Tom's niece, Kelly, in the family room and soon Kelly came and asked me, "Janet, do you have anything for heartburn? Your mom is complaining of indigestion." I didn't think too much about it and simply gave her something I had in the cabinet. Later that evening Tom took my mom home and as far as I know she wasn't complaining of any further upset. The following day my brother and sister and I all stopped by my mom's house and she mentioned she still wasn't feeling good, although she didn't go into any specifics. My sister didn't seem to be too alarmed so I guess I wasn't either. Tom's brother was leaving to go back to Oklahoma that day so I was going with Tom to say goodbye to him. Before we left we called my aunt, who lives just a couple of blocks away, and asked her to keep an eye on my mom for us. My cousin from Florida even stopped by later that day, but when she didn't answer the door he just assumed she was sleeping.

We got home about the same time Jeff arrived from school. He seemed worried and said, "Mom, there's a message on the recorder from Grandma, and she really sounds sick." All three of us jumped in the car. We found her pale and very weak and rather than calling an ambulance, we drove to the hospital. My sister and brother were waiting when we arrived. We were very fortunate that the heart specialist team was there so she was evaluated immediately, and they performed an angioplasty. Afterwards when the nurse wheeled her out into the hallway, she looked pretty good. Her color was much less pale and she seemed comfortable. Then all of a sudden the nurse said, "How are you doing, Helen?" There was no response. Her eyes had been open, but then they just shut. My sister and I were really jolted; we thought she died right there. They rushed her up to the intensive care unit and attached her to all those machines with the beeping that just drove me crazy.

The chaplain sat down with us while they got my mom settled in the unit. Her general practitioner came to the waiting room as well, and when he saw me he gave me a hug. I remember him saying, somewhat jokingly, "Is there a God?" He knew we had just lost Jill, and I think he felt my mom was in pretty bad shape.

My mom had a stroke earlier that last August and had gone through rehab for a time. We imagine that she had another stroke after the angioplasty. I don't know all the details even to this day, but I'm sure the doctors explained it to my sister. After just losing Jill, how much more could I handle? Of course at that time we didn't know what the outcome would be with my mom. We understood that she was very sick, but we didn't anticipate she would die.

I went to the hospital every day. The nurses knew we had just buried our daughter. All they would have to do is look at me, and I could tell they knew. About ninety percent of the time my mom appeared asleep, but I would go in and pat her hand and say, "Mom, Janet's here." She would shudder when I said that, and I felt I was upsetting her. No one could know what she was thinking but it broke my heart, so then I started sitting with her but not saying anything. I just couldn't bear to see her shudder at my voice. So many things were left unspoken after the tragedy with Jill. She was a part of so many.

Everyone seemed to be holding up. My sister never talked about her feelings or her problems, even in usual circumstances. My brother visited often as well as the grandchildren. I don't think Jeff came up very much – he didn't like hospitals. They made him uncomfortable and of course we didn't force him after all he had just gone through. So therefore there we were, living through the tragedy of losing Jill and yet up at the hospital every night with my mom, while Jeff was home alone.

Days turned into weeks and she remained in intensive care. During that time the numbness from Jill's loss just carried over. I merely progressed from one bad situation to another. I was performing the motions of daily life, knowing that I should be there for my mom, so I was. I was able to think, but mostly from my heart. It was a very emotional time, but my tears were for Jill and not my mom. For her I was just trying to be strong. I had to keep going.

The numbness seemed to continue for the first two weeks or so after Jill's death and in a way it truly was a thankful numbness. Afterwards, the feelings that had been locked in frozen silence began to thaw and gush into my senses, especially in the quiet moments. It was then I could feel the desolation of my soul. In the days and weeks after Jill's death everyone else was going back to normal, but there was no "normal" for me anymore. No way to go back – that's just the way it was.

I began to feel angry. Ever since Jill found out she would have to drive all the way to Michigan City for her nursing clinicals

I had been angry. There was another facility much closer to home – why hadn't the school figured out a way to send the students who commuted closer to their homes? That highway was always icy in winter. That was the anger I was feeling, if in fact you could call it anger. It was more a disappointment in people's judgment. The girls had made it to their very last day. I had already been breathing easier.

We had a lot of questions about the actual accident, but because we were so emotionally distraught we didn't seek out any answers. We never made any calls to either the university or the parents of the two surviving girls, and those parents never made an attempt to contact us either. We never received even a card from them nor did we ever meet them. Still to this day we don't know if the girls were being careless – it was their last day before spring break. We wonder why the van wasn't able to swerve to miss the car. So many questions, yet at the time everyone was in the same emotional state that we were. I never wanted to bring more pain to people.

Adrienne, the girl who was driving the car, was in the hospital at the same time my mother was. I wrote a note to her saying I was hoping that she was feeling better and asked the nurses to give it to her. I didn't think seeing me would do her much good as I was too distraught at the time. I wanted her to know that we wished her well, though.

Tom went back to work after a week. I knew he was hurting but financial responsibilities had to be met. Tom and I never really talked much about our loss. We didn't want to keep reopening each other's wounds. I am sure Tom tried his best to protect me from continued pain – especially with my mom in the hospital. If you should ever know someone who is going through the loss of a child, talk to them about it. If you bring it up a couple of times and they don't respond, then let it be. Everyone deals with it differently - but at least try.

Who was I talking to at the time? No one, except for small talk like, "How are you doing?" "Fine, thank you." Have you ever walked up to somebody and said, "How are you doing?" and then stand there for an hour or two listening about all their aches and pains? People may really want to know but how much are you going to tell them? I just felt that I had to be strong and deal with it. It was my loss. I didn't want anyone to feel sorry for me and I didn't want to put my burden on them. This was something Tom and I had to live through even though I knew others were hurting too. People were always welcomed to come and go at our house and talk, but everyone shied away from talking about Jill because they knew how emotional I was. People don't really know what to say to you anyway. Like when you go to a funeral home, all you can say is, "I'm very sorry." Everybody certainly knows that's not enough but what are you going to say? Nobody has any answers.

My family and our closest friends still hovered over us in the weeks following Jill's death, particularly when my mom was in the hospital. I felt that the ones who weren't keeping close were handling the loss in their own way. I did learn, however, that when you're the parent who's dealing with the loss of a child, you're the one who has to take the first step forward in talking to people. I would have thought people would automatically come up and say something. They don't – they wait for you to take the initiative. They're reluctant to even say hello to you. Even in a restaurant or at the store – you walk by someone you know and exchange niceties, and then you see them whispering about you after you walk on. They're afraid to talk to you because they don't want to hurt you or make you cry, and everyone forgets how to act or carry on a conversation. That puts pressure on the parent to get the ball rolling or else there's dead silence. People just don't know.

I remember some family members feeling bad after Jill's death because we didn't ask them to help with certain things, like writing out thank you cards for example. Honestly, we didn't think about it. If people were at our house at the time and they offered to help with something, that's how it got done. We didn't invite people to do anything specific. Whoever came forward, that's how the chips fell.

A couple of weeks after the funeral I had to start thinking about going back to work. Up until that time I was just trying to get adjusted to life again – getting up in the morning, getting dressed, talking to people. Having Jeff kept me going. I had to try and reestablish normalcy for his sake. Finally, it was just a matter of realizing I had to go back to work. My supervisor encouraged me too. She declared, "You're going to have to just pick a day, Janet." And that's what I did. I started back on a Monday. There were a lot of tears that first week and honestly I think it was just as hard for my co-workers to have me back as it was for me to be there. They had been as devastated by Jill's loss as I was and didn't know how to handle the situation any better than I did. They were kind and understanding, certainly, but still strained. Actually going back to work was helpful. I very slowly got back into a comfortable routine, and the busy atmosphere became my therapy.

On March 22, I went to visit my mom in intensive care as usual. She seemed to be stable; she had in fact rallied for a short time previously and even made some attempts at communicating by chalkboard, but now she was comatose. I left the hospital that night and a few hours later her heart stopped. The doctors were able to bring her back once, but afterward my sister told them no more. My sister's call to me later that evening was expected.

She was admitted to intensive care on February 29 and died there on March 22, 1994. That was eighteen years to the day that my dad had died. I felt in my heart she had been waiting for that.

# 33

# Tom

After Jill's funeral we really needed time to relax and absorb all that had happened. That, of course, wasn't to be.

Janet's mom was gradually becoming weaker throughout the previous months, but I do believe Jill's death pushed her over. Not only was there the stress of the loss itself but there was the funeral, the out-of-town company – all the activity in general with so many people around.

When her mom was admitted to ICU, Janet's emotions went from the fire to the frying pan. We had just buried our daughter and now she had to deal with the possibility of losing her mother. Janet is stronger than a lot of people would imagine. Her emotions are always at the forefront, but she will do what needs to be done even through turmoil and tears. Janet may be hurting unbearably but she will go on, whereas many others might give up.

I was off work the entire week after Jill's funeral. To go back to work was difficult, but it was something I felt had to be done. Whether it was a week or a month, I had to go back, so why put it off? Once I was sure Janet was able to function, I decided to start back.

It wasn't as difficult for me to go back to the mill as it was for Janet to go back to her office. There are so many people at a steel mill; I didn't have the small, family-type environment that she did. There wasn't time to sit and dwell about what happened – we had to start work. In that way it was therapeutic, keeping my mind occupied and off my sorrow. I did have a few people come up to me and say how sorry they were, but otherwise it was business as usual.

Janet went to the hospital every night to visit her mom, and I went with her when my work schedule allowed. I believe after those few weeks we expected her death and to a certain degree we were prepared for it. I tried my best to be a leaning post for Janet, but my own strengths were still drained from Jill's loss. It was then I most admired and appreciated Janet's fortitude. People may not think they can get through a certain situation, but they can and do.

I always felt as long as Janet and I had each other and could reinforce each other, we could pull through. I know that statistics might show some of the highest divorce rates occur after the loss of a child, and I can understand that. It's because the loss has been so great that many people just wouldn't care what happened afterwards. They stop working at their marriage – stop everything, but relationships are the only things that *do* matter. Nothing else does - not the house, the cars - nothing. Everything else can be fixed or replaced, but you can't fix death. The hardest thing about death is there's nothing you can do about it. You can't go back in time and change things; you can't bring that person back to life.

About a week after we lost Jill, I had a dream. Actually it was more than just a dream. Dreams aren't real, but this was real, although I can't imagine people would believe me. I dreamt that I was in our house and Jill was there with me. As soon as I saw her I started to cry, and she said to me, "Dad, why are you crying? It's okay, it's okay." Then she hugged me. That's all there was, but it was real, so real. She was there, and she was her whole self, not injured or scarred. Afterwards I sat up in bed and cried almost hysterically. I was upset because I didn't talk to her, I didn't make the most of my time with her. All I could do was cry. I got a chance to see her and hold her, but it was over too soon.

I later learned that that same night, Betty said that she felt a cold hand press against her hand while she was in bed, and she knew that Jill was there.

About two weeks after Jill's death, after the spring break at the University, a memorial service was held for the three girls who died. It was very touching to all of us, as about eight hundred people attended from the school and community. That was the first time Janet and I were able to meet and talk with the two girls who survived the crash. Janet and I walked in the chapel and saw them as they saw us. We advanced slowly towards each other and Adrienne, the driver, was still on crutches. We talked together but Adrienne was having a very difficult time of it. She spoke through tears and we tried to be supportive of her. There was no blame, no sarcasm, but of course everyone was tense. We realized that both girls had a lot to deal with at the time and probably still do.

We never met or even heard from the families of the two surviving girls, but the other families who lost their daughters were there. We all talked about how we were doing and there were a lot of tears. It was another hard thing to do, to go to that service, and we were all so tired from those past two weeks. We found out that Kim Pressel had just lost her father a couple of months prior to the crash. She had just come back to school after grieving for him. The other mother, Mrs. Van Dyke, explained that she herself was taking some nursing courses near Indianapolis and was planning on transferring up to Valparaiso University the following year. She and her daughter were going to get an apartment together and finish up school. She was experiencing great difficulty being at the memorial service, but that was to be expected. None of us wanted to be there.

Overall, the service was both positive and helpful. So many students came through the receiving line and expressed their sympathies. We later learned the University had lowered the flag to half-mast for the first time in decades. The nursing school also did an etching of the girl's faces and hung a plaque in the lobby area of the nursing hall. Later, a flowering pear tree was planted on the grounds by the School of Nursing, and it blooms three times a year to symbolize the three nursing students.

After the service a luncheon was held and as it turned out Jeff was not able to sit at the table Janet and I shared with the other parents. He was seated at a table along with the President of the University. Jeff told me afterward the President had asked him what his plans were after graduating high school, and he had told him engineering. The President didn't miss a chance to recruit a new student and started telling Jeff what a great engineering program VU had. Jeff listened patiently and at the end thanked him but said he was going to Purdue!

In the weeks following Jill's death I was still in aftershock. From the moment someone you love dies, it doesn't get any easier. You don't just say, "Okay, she's dead, and now I have to start over again – a new life." It just doesn't work that way. You never get back to normal again. Normal is forever gone.

Time doesn't cure all. Sometimes, the more time that passes, the more you miss the one you lost. It's almost worse, yet in a different way. More things remind you of them - songs, pictures, everyday life. Perhaps some people find it easier to forget, but not me. I will carry that grief with me forever.

I was thinking about Jill almost constantly at that time. I would be talking to someone about her and they would tell me something I didn't know, like the time she helped another nursing student with math, and Jill wasn't great in math to begin with! Nevertheless, she took the time to help. If we would go to someone's house and their kids were there, it reminded us all because Jill was missed. Even the simplest things, like a commercial on TV with a teddy bear in it, reminded us that we had buried Jill with her teddy bear. Anything can set off the memory – even a silly commercial. I was surrounded by these kinds of reminders so it was impossible not to think of her. That's what we would live with for the rest of our lives. It never goes away.

I handled my grief by just going along with it. I tried to keep it in its place, although a lot of times it didn't stay there, but I had to try because otherwise I couldn't function. I knew that whatever came along I would just have to deal with it – to keep myself out of a mental hospital. I think some people would get to that point if they let it, but you can't let it. You need to get back into the system. Whether we live our lives happily or unhappily, we still have to live, until we die as well.

What does it feel like to lose a daughter? Well, if you could think of the worst thing that could happen to you – the absolute worst thing – it would be much worse than that.

# 34

# Janet

Many times when someone dies, especially an older person who has been suffering or in a coma, it's normal to feel a sense of relief at their passing. Now they are at peace; they don't have to suffer any more, but with my mom, I wasn't feeling much relief. What I was feeling was, "Oh my God, not another death." It was devastation all over again.

My brother and sister made most of the decisions on arrangements, but I did go along and help pick out her casket and flowers. I would never have walked away and not done what was needed. I do what I have to do and get through it. I may take a dive afterward, but I'll get back on my feet as best as I can. You don't have a choice. If every parent who lost a child had a choice, that child would be back at home.

We did not choose the same funeral home as we had with Jill, and I really think that was for the best. We had just been there for our daughter; it was too soon to go back for my mother.

Diane had made the comment to me that she didn't think I was taking Jill's death very hard. That really caught me off guard – how could I not be taking it hard? I think what she meant is because I'm so emotional, I held up better than she thought. During Jill's service I was teary-eyed but the emotions that churned within were trapped tight. In fact even I couldn't understand how I could actually do that – talk to people and just be a little teary-eyed. It seemed we just fell into a routine, with people coming through the line so fast and all saying the same thing. "We're sorry." "Thank you for coming." How could I not be overwhelmingly hysterical? Some people say that's where God helps you.

My mom's funeral, however, was a different situation. I had more time to think, to reflect on what was happening, because a smaller group of people were in attendance. That's when all the events of the past month came to a head for me. At the church service I tried so hard not to cry, but I think they could hear me throughout the church. I was trying to hold back the sobs but there's no holding back a roaring river. I cried for Jill and I cried for my mom. I cried for Tom and Jeff and for me because of the pain we would carry forever. I cried for our world which for the moment seemed to make no sense and have no fairness or compassion.

My friends and family rallied to our sides yet again. They all came back to town to go through it once more. It's hard to lose a mother. Mothers are the backbone of a family, providing strength and cohesiveness. I always thought that grieving for Jill would have been easier if my mother had been there in the months that followed. But would it have been? Nobody knows. She was close to Jill and of course I was too, so maybe we could have helped each other.

I really should have taken the time to sit down and talk with Jeff about losing Grandma. He would just go to his room or watch TV, not saying much at all. With my mom I regretted not talking about Jill, with Jeff I regretted not talking about both Jill and my mom. I thought he was doing okay, but he probably wasn't. He was struggling just like the rest of us. In a way, I never had the opportunity to grieve for my mom, and maybe Jeff didn't either. Our grief for Jill was overwhelming.

++++++++++++++++++++++++++++++++++++++++++

Prior to Jill's death the four of us had planned a trip to Florida along with Tom's brother Jerry and his wife and children. We were going in March in conjunction with the Hoosier Hysteria basketball games in Indianapolis, which we attended every year. Tom and the rest of the family felt that we should go ahead with our plans, thinking it would be good to get away. My mom was buried on a Friday, and we were to leave that Saturday for the games. Jerry and Joene decided to leave Friday night with their children and Jeff, and Tom and I would drive down to Indianapolis on Saturday and meet them there.

After the funeral Jeff went from the cemetery to home to change clothes for the trip to Indianapolis. He then came to the church for the dinner, planning to leave with Jerry directly from there. Well, the last time we all went to the games, the kids had lunch at a Hooter's restaurant. Jeff bought a t-shirt there and sure enough he put it on when he went home to change. He showed up in the church basement wearing a Hooter's car-racing t-shirt after all the local clergy had recently fought against our town getting a Hooter's restaurant. I just couldn't believe it, yet there he was – big as life. I was speechless, but everyone just chuckled quietly and said leave him be. He probably didn't even realize that he was being "politically incorrect." He just put on a clean t-shirt!

I can't say I really enjoyed myself on that trip, but it was good to get away even though it was difficult. There were a lot of tears on the way and I hated for my sister-in-law and her kids to have to deal with that. It was probably very good for Jeff – it helped to reestablish some normalcy. Once we got back home it was like we had never left. Reality just picked up where it had left off.

We did little with Jill's room immediately after her loss. I didn't really need the space for anything so there was no impetus to change anything. I packed up some of her clothes and gave them away, but otherwise everything was just as she had left it.

We kept her door closed at first. I guess it was easier not to see her things every time we walked by. It was better to shut it off, not that that was ever entirely possible. Some people who have lost a child have since told me that they packed up all their belongings – even their pictures – and put them away. That may be good for them but to me it would be like trying to forget they ever existed. I didn't want to forget her. So, everything was left the way it was. Eventually, we started opening her door again. I would even go in and look around, or pick up this or that, and yes it was comforting to be able to touch the things she had touched, but we didn't keep her room with the intention of making it a memorial. We would even give things away if anyone asked for something specific, like a friend of hers who had gone to ballet with her asked me for the pair of ceramic ballet slippers that were hanging on her wall. I was glad to give them to her. Out of everything, those caught her eye, so they obviously meant something to her. Later our neighbor Carol, who was Jill's confirmation sponsor, asked if she could have one of Jill's music boxes so I pulled all of them out and let her choose the one she wanted.

Although it didn't happen right away, gradually I came to feel closer to Diane than ever before. She knew more of what we were going through because she had lost Larry when he was so young. When something like that happens to two people, it just draws you closer. Although I never really had a conversation with her about my feelings or how I was doing, there was a knowingness between the two of us. She was a support system for me. I had a lot of support, but she was the only one who had survived that kind of loss.

Surprisingly, I didn't suffer any panic attacks after Jill's loss. While my mom was sick, I was still in the meat of things. The panic attacks usually come later, after the immediate stress has lessened and the new reality begins to choke your thoughts, but with my mom in the hospital my adrenalin kicked in, and I knew what I had to do to keep going.

As slow as you can imagine it, the grief does get better, although "better" is not really the right word. Who could ever get over losing a child? You can't. You just learn over time to deal with it in a different way. You handle it differently when you're around people – not as emotionally. So it doesn't become better, just more manageable. It becomes part of your day, like your secret companion that everyone knows really exists.

# 35

# Tom

It only stands to reason that Janet had a very difficult time at her mom's funeral. Why wouldn't she? She was still very much in the after-effects of Jill and now she was trying her best to deal with her mom's death. It wasn't like her mom had cancer and had been sick for a year. All of a sudden she went from being relatively healthy to dying. So it was traumatic, yes, although I never reached the point where I wondered how or if she had the strength to pull through this latest heartbreak. Nevertheless, her sobs in church that day tore through me like steel spikes.

We also had Jeff to be concerned about. During the month after Jill's death he had gotten back into the school routine. Being with his friends seemed to help him so we encouraged that. He never talked much about what he felt and he only told you what he wanted you to know. When he did speak of Jill it was in a joking way, and hopefully those light memories helped ease the pain he was feeling or at least helped him remember better days. He seemed to handle Grandma's death in the same way as Jill's – quiet, solemn. He stayed close to his cousins, kids his own age. We never pushed him to participate in anything that made him feel uncomfortable.

After the funeral we had the practical things to take care of, and it was cathartic to have something to throw ourselves into. We worked at her mom's house along with the rest of the family and got it ready for sale. Her dog had eaten the edges of a few cabinets and tore up part of the flooring, so we redid all of that. We fixed the back door, went through the whole house and painted, and actually it looked very nice when we got done with it. The kids split up everything of hers that they wanted. I remember lots of Elvis Presley albums – she was a big fan.

Once that task was accomplished it was a matter of reestablishing our family life, but this time without Jill. We worked, came home, ate supper. Jeff was a junior in high school and his school activities kept him busy. I don't think I became more protective of Jeff after losing Jill, but I do think I was more involved with him after that. I appreciated him more. We would talk – I would tell him things and he would tell me things. Sometimes we would talk about our feelings or what was going on. I would talk about what was important, like schooling or grades, and he would say, "Don't worry about it, Dad, everything's taken care of." I was realizing that people have to keep close to each other, especially their kids. I had always been working. I had tried to be as involved as I could in their lives but there were a lot of times it wasn't possible because of the shift work.

Otherwise, the three of us did what we normally did. We never did very much! We led a quiet life, but without Jill the house was even quieter. We took it day by day, handling whatever came up. We didn't sit around and cry every night, but we had our times when we would sit in the stillness of the evening and just talk. We kept participating in life. You can't stop doing that no matter how you feel.

People really didn't know too much about our personal grief. It's not something they felt at ease talking about in general conversation. Death makes people uncomfortable, especially the death of someone so young. Sorrow makes people uncomfortable – I guess that's why everyone works so hard to dispel it, or at least detour around it. It's human nature, but we were all hurting. You could try to take that momentary detour, but eventually it led you right back to Jill.

Both of our families were very supportive during this time. No one stopped talking to us and that was most helpful of all. They didn't leave us by ourselves. Even if they just called to talk about simple things – Janet's sister and brother began calling every day. We talked about how our days went and sometimes Jill would come up in the conversation, other times not. Small talk, but it kept the family close.

We didn't do anything to Jill's bedroom – didn't even think about doing anything. You know how you see in the movies where they open an old door and the room inside has cobwebs spun over everything? Well, it wasn't quite that bad, but I did want to preserve everything the way it was. I suppose I didn't want to erase the memories. If we erased her room we might erase the memories, and then it wouldn't be the same. As it was, I could open the door and look in and remember the way things were. We just couldn't bring ourselves to change that.

# 36

# Janet

Our church and community had shown us phenomenal support after Jill's death. It was unbelievable how the congregation had gathered for us and how the community rallied around us, and we had been amazed at the people who came and stood by and did without asking.

We did not go to church the Sunday following Jill's funeral and after a while not going to church became the more comfortable choice for me. I think I stayed away mainly because I couldn't imagine sitting there crying for the whole hour. I knew people would try to approach me and talk to me, and frankly I didn't have the energy at that time to say anymore "thank you's." I guess what I was probably doing – which was wrong – was avoiding the people who had been there to support me. I just didn't want to keep crying every time I saw someone. I was very concerned about putting stress on other people. I always felt this was something Tom and I had to live through but our friends didn't, and I didn't want my sorrow spilling over on them.

I suppose I stayed away because of the songs, too. They triggered memories, and if I could hide even a little while from the pain those memories stirred, I would.

Occasionally I would go to church, like when there was a special mass for Jill. I remember one lady who directed the teen club that Jill had been a part of. When there was a memorial mass for Jill she would lead the songs or do the reading and when she passed me, she would press a small token in my hand and squeeze. Of course there were other people who didn't know what to say to me, other than small talk. They were just as afraid to approach me as I was afraid to be among them. So I suppose there were many reasons I pulled back from Sunday mass.

Yes, I was angry at God for Jill's accident. Why did she have to die? Every day in the newspapers there are stories about people who couldn't pass the alcohol test yet survived their accidents. Or how about the drug abusers who overdosed, yet lived? You have to wonder why He is taking the good and leaving the problems for us to deal with. But that's sitting in judgment and I shouldn't do that either, because even though that person's a drug addict or an alcoholic, he has parents who love and care for him too. If that happened to him, it would be tragic for his family as well. Then you think of the elderly in nursing homes who have no one left to visit them and only wish God would spare them further agony. Why wouldn't He take someone like that who may be in pain from the disease they're suffering with? He took a young, healthy body instead.

I was in a quandary. I didn't know what to think about my faith at that time, and I will always have those questions. I can't comprehend how Jill, who was respected in the community in which she lived and who routinely went out of her way to help people, could have been taken. Why? She was not selfish; she was an asset to the community. Our towns need people who care, who genuinely take an interest in people's lives or step outside their immediate circle to help someone else. Some people believe that everything happens for a reason – to make you a better person. If Jill had survived, it seems to me she would have been a gift in our world. The world lacks so much compassion and there is so much greed and ruination. So you wonder. With all the other garbage that is going on, why wouldn't He let her stay and lead a long life? You could see the direction she was going, and she had so many good qualities, so much to give.

Some people have said to me, "Well, maybe Jill was going to have poor health and God saved her from that or something more disastrous." As a human being I can't deal with anything more than the fact that Jill is no longer a part of our lives. She isn't here to come home at night and have dinner with us. She isn't here to talk to, and she's not here to love.

I couldn't even pray to God for my own help and support. I would try, and then I would think, "Why am I even asking?" I didn't think He would answer my prayers. I have friends who have lost people close to them, and they claim many times you don't see the answers because you're still so deep in grieving. You're not permitting yourself to see beyond that. Your mind is not in a state that allows you to see.

Eventually, I did go back to praying; I prayed for Jeff's safety. I prayed because it was a natural part of me, as much as I wanted to begrudge God and make Him the fault. I still had that connection and I didn't want to lose total contact. There was that part of me that was used to saying prayers and was used to asking for the safety of my family. Maybe God was still looking after us. Maybe we could get through this.

Slowly, we returned to some normalcy. We turned all of our attentions toward Jeff and tried our best to protect him from our sorrows. He was a junior in high school – he had his senior year, graduation, college – all of that was in front of him.

Jeff never expressed much about his grief. One of the other mothers who lost a daughter in the accident had a son too, and she asked me if Jeff ever talked about Jill. I told her no, or only in a joking way, and she said her son never expressed much either. A time later when we were together with them I asked her son why he didn't talk about his sister, and he said there really wasn't much to say. What happened, happened. What can you say? The loss is always there. That's probably how Jeff felt, too.

There were nights when Tom would be working and Jeff would hear me crying, even though I tried to keep it down. He would come in the bedroom and lay on top of the covers and talk. "Are you okay, Mom?" "Yes, Jeff, I'm okay." I kept it to small talk. He was very sensitive to other people, yet I didn't want him burdened with my grief.

We went to the cemetery pretty regularly, especially in the summer. My sister-in-law had asked if she could plant flowers on Jill's grave, and I never wanted to deny people if they wanted to contribute something that was meaningful to them. She would always plant in pinks and lavenders - Jill's favorites – and after that Tom and I would maintain it. We put in a vigil candle and kept that lit for special occasions, and my sister and brother were very faithful in bringing flowers. Once my brother brought roses, and he told me he pricked his finger on one of the thorns. He joked, "You know I bet Sissy was up there laughing at me. I bet she thought that was really funny."

The summer after Jill's death we stayed low-keyed. Jeff worked for the Parks Department again and I was happy he was out in the fresh air. He would mow the lawn, running over the plants occasionally I'm sure. I worked in my garden. I think that's the one place that offered me the most peace – just working out there silently with my flowers. My mind was free; I listened to the birds and relaxed. I saw farmers go by on their tractors, families riding their bikes, bikers out on their Harley's. It amazed me what a cross section of the world you can find right in your backyard. I waved to just about anybody who went by, any time I saw I had their attention. Jill would have done that too.

Family and friends were treating us normally again by the time summer arrived, and that was okay with us. We didn't get a lot of visitors. I think I probably needed the solitude to try to think things through. I didn't have to concentrate on what I said, and I didn't have to hold back from crying. There were many times when I would just sit in peace.

People shied away from talking about Jill because they didn't know how, and when things were happening in their own lives with their own children they were reluctant to share those with me. I finally had to say to a few, "Listen, those are happy times for you, and I have to live with that. I'm happy for you, too." Hopefully, they appreciated knowing how I felt.

I went to my cousin's once and she was showing pictures of her daughter who had gone to Prom and she said to me, "Janet, you don't have to look at those pictures."

"Why not?" I replied. "She's beautiful and that's a happy time for her, and I'm happy for her!" Just because my daughter was gone didn't mean I wasn't going to be happy for all the other parents who still had theirs. They were due their happiness. It is possible to feel joy amidst overwhelming sadness. It is possible to be a part of life.

# 37

# Tom

After Jill died, I kept going to church – for a while. Then one day as I sat there during the service, it just hit me. I didn't know why I was there. All of a sudden it didn't make sense. What the priest was saying didn't correspond to what I knew to be real life. So I got up and walked out.

The church had been very supportive to our whole family after Jill's death. My feelings didn't have anything to do with the priest or the congregation or anything like that. It's the doctrine I had problems with. The Church talks about life and death – death is supposed to be the next, natural step after life, when you will be with God. Your faith should allow you to feel contentment after someone has died, knowing that person was now in God's hands. I just couldn't do that. I didn't feel I was angry. I didn't feel mad at God. Many believe that God doesn't control what happens to people – people take control of their own destinies. So you can't be mad at Him – what's the point? Although I used to tell people, when they asked me why I didn't go to church, that God and I weren't getting along at the time. It wasn't that I didn't love God or even that I had stopped praying to Him. At the time, we just weren't seeing eye to eye.

I didn't feel Jill had been taken specifically to hurt me. I felt it was just something that happened – a terrible accident. Yet, all my life I had heard about miracles and guardian angels and how God saved people. Where was Jill's angel? Didn't she have one?

I understood the doctrines of the Church; I just couldn't sit there and participate the way I was feeling. I felt the doctrines the priests were teaching, even though they might be true for everyone else, weren't true for Janet and I. I think Janet felt the same as I did. She had gone to mass even less than I did after losing Jill.

Nevertheless, to a certain degree I'm sure religion played a part in helping us survive our loss. We did get some strength from our faith, but not one-hundred percent. It did help us to understand more about life and death and to prepare for what's beyond the moment or the lifetime. It gave me hope that Jill was in a good place. I'm sure everyone feels differently about these things. One instance I know of where a couple lost their son, they actually felt joy after the funeral because their son was in heaven and happy. I couldn't feel that way. It may even be true, but all I knew for a certainty is how I felt – then and now. I miss Jill, and I want her to be with me. I feel we didn't have enough time together. I wasn't allowed to see her grow and prosper and succeed in what she was trying to accomplish. I wanted to see her live a good life, but she didn't have a chance to finish what she started, and neither did I, neither did Janet. We were robbed. I think that's what it is more than anything else. We were robbed.

We would go back to church every now and again, like when they had special masses for Jill, but never on a regular basis. I still believed in God. I just chose not to practice a formalized religion. And Jeff – well he was never one for church, even though he had his faith, too. He would go only because he was with us. After Jill was killed, he didn't want anything to do with church.

++++++++++++++++++++++++++++++++++++++++++

I don't remember much about the summer after Jill's death. I was working as usual and we just got back into our routine, although it wasn't normal like when Jill was with us. You do what you have to do.

I found myself thinking a lot about Jill. It wasn't continuous; it wasn't consuming. I would be busy doing different things and my mind was on what I was doing, but then the memories would start rolling in like an early fog, and I would be thinking of Jill. That happened many times at work, especially when we had downtime. Various things would remind me of her, like when a particular song came on the radio. Different songs triggered so many different memories. It seemed like there was quite a bit that reminded me of Jill, actually. I tried to keep myself busy. The busier I was, the less my mind wandered and my heart ached, though it was often wearisome to concentrate.

Initially, going to the cemetery was very difficult. I was driving there to look at a stone, yet so many emotions were evoked by that stone. It never stopped me from going, though, and we would go often. Later, I always felt a sense of peace knowing that I had been there and talked to her, even though that unending sense of loss soon crept in and overshadowed the peace.

During that summer our family and close friends treated us pretty much the same as they always had. Sometimes they would go out of their way to make sure everything was going okay. At first they shied away from talking about Jill until they saw that we weren't afraid to talk about her. I think most people would assume we didn't want to mention her and stir up the hurt, but both Janet and I were able and willing to talk about Jill and that put everyone else at ease.

Come the following September, Jeff would be a high school senior, though I'm not at all sure that excited him. He was looking beyond that and planning for college. He knew what he wanted. He was just like Jill.

# 38

# Janet

In February of 1995 I turned fifty, and I didn't think it would bother me, but it did. Fifty meant you were going towards sixty. Forty going towards fifty wasn't so bad. And fifty didn't really bother me until I went to the grocery store. The check-out girl asked me if I had a senior citizen's discount card! I said no, but she gave me the discount anyway! Then a couple of weeks later, I went back to the grocery store and there was an older woman, probably in her seventies, and we were both looking in the cookie aisle. I couldn't find any cookies I wanted, so I went around to the next aisle and we eventually met again. She said, "I noticed you looking at the cookies. You couldn't find anything you wanted, huh?"

"Well, I tried but I couldn't!" I answered.

She laughed, "But we don't want to bake any, do we?"

"No, not really," I told her.

"Do you live alone?" she asked me. Like she's already assuming I'm widowed!

I'm thinking, "I'll be darned! Maybe it's because of my gray hair." I hear people talk about my aunt, who is ninety-one, and they say she looks great, but I go to the grocery store and they offer me senior citizen discounts or assume I'm widowed! I came home and called Diane and told her, "Diane, I think we ought to dye my hair tonight." But she was ready for bed by that time so we didn't. I thought, "Good grief. Nobody ever says that to my sister." From then on I felt like sending my sister to the grocery store for me. I had never felt I was vain, but at the time it really did bother me. I told my ninety-one-year-old aunt about it and she just laughed. Maybe she knew something I didn't.

Jeff's senior year of high school was pretty uneventful. He was quiet, he didn't run around too much, and there were no puppy-loves - until Kristen came into the picture, that is. Kristen picked Jeff out and over time the feelings became mutual. She was quite the tomboy, into tennis and other sports. It was nothing to see her and Tom and Jeff sitting in the living room watching games on TV. She knew all the teams and got very focused on the plays. She was a very pretty girl, even in her baseball cap, which she always wore even though her mother hated it. We liked her very much.

Kristen asked Jeff to the Senior Prom. Now Jeff, mind you, was pretty tight with a dollar. He was also a fairly lucky kid. Kristen was in National Honor Society and that year they had a drawing for all expenses paid to the Prom. She won! So Jeff didn't have to pay for anything except dinner! The limo, his tux, the flowers – everything was taken care of. That was right up his alley.

Jeff's High School Graduation with his parents

When graduation came along, Jeff chose to have his party in our backyard rather than in a hall like Jill. It wasn't a very large party, just close friends, but it was nice and we all had a good time. Jeff certainly had no regrets about leaving high school behind. He was ready to move on. You know, I don't remember what we bought him for his graduation gift, but it was probably conservative! We were always conservative, and I regret that a little. I never wanted to spoil our kids, but if I had it to do all over again I would spoil them rotten.

My sister's second son, Kevin, was in engineering at Purdue University, and I think he influenced Jeff quite a bit. Jeff had always been mechanically inclined, however, so it didn't surprise me a bit when he chose to go into an engineering program. He also picked Purdue, though I don't know how much of that was Kevin's persuasiveness, but he sure was happy when he got his letter of acceptance. Lafayette was only an hour away from home, and he had decided to attend the main campus and live at the dorm. He wanted that campus experience. I always used to tell Jill that spending a semester or two on campus should be part of the curriculum. I thought it was a good learning tool to go along with their education. Some friends of Jeff's were headed to Purdue, too - even Kristen, and of course Kevin was there if Jeff ever needed him. They didn't have a lot of contact with each other, as Kevin was three years ahead of Jeff, but whenever Jeff had questions about which courses were best, or if he ever needed anything, Kevin was always there for him.

It didn't bother me that he was going to be an hour away. There were evenings when I would get off work and Tom and I would hop in the car and drive down to see him. It was a beautiful ride in the spring and fall. We would open up the sun roof, let the wind blow through our hair and head on down to West Lafayette. We'd have dinner with Jeff and then get back on the highway towards home. I felt comfortable too because it was a straight drive for Jeff when he wanted to come home.

I remember every time he would leave the house to drive back to school he would say goodbye to us at the door, but once he left the house he would never look back. It was as though he knew he had to go, even though he didn't want to. I would stand on the porch and wave to him, but he never turned around to see.

Tom and I now had an empty house. After losing Jill we could tell a big difference. Not many phone calls after that! Then when Jeff left, it was extremely quiet. No coming and going. It was hard to get used to.

Whenever Jeff did come home, I felt that I had to respect the fact that he was used to being on his own now. I couldn't expect him to abide by the old rules, like being in by midnight. He was his own person now. I just said, "Please be careful when you go out." I always left the upstairs hall light on for him. When I woke up and saw the hall light off, I knew he had come home. I thought of him as an adult.

He was still quiet and kept a lot of things inside. Even though he didn't verbalize his thoughts, I could see things on his face. He always wore this little grin that made me think, "Okay, is he up to good or no good?" I called it his shitty grin. He kept me guessing.

When he did come home, he would bring every single piece of his dirty laundry with him. I washed clothes all weekend, which he thought was so funny. "Hey Mom, I brought something for you!"

"Gee Jeff, how nice!" He and I would exchange smiles – that's how he showed his love, in his smile. I always knew. That was his joke on me, even though he would end up helping me! Probably because I wasn't fast enough for him!

His freshman year he spent in the dorm. He was never a complainer and Tom and I didn't know till the end of the year how uncomfortable he was there. His roommate wasn't very clean and was just there for the party. He played his guitar halfway through the night, never changed his sheets, and slept half the day. Jeff never mentioned those things until the year was over. That's how he was. Knowing it would shortly be all over, he would just deal with it.

*No Words*

    The second semester of his freshman year was the first time Jeff had been away from home on the anniversary of Jill's death. He had taken Kristen to a dance that night and then back to her sorority house. Then he jumped in his car and shot down the highway to Merrillville. Tom and I didn't know this; we just assumed he was in West Lafayette and would go back to his dorm after the dance. We never thought about him coming home, although we had thought about Jill all day. We had gone to the cemetery and had wondered how Jeff was handling being away, but we figured he was with Kristen and she knew the situation so he wouldn't be alone. Then, about 1:00 AM, we heard the garage door go up and Tom went downstairs. Jeff walked in the house, still in his suit, and Tom exclaimed, "What are you doing home?"

    "I went to the cemetery," Jeff said. Here it was pitch dark, and he had gone to the cemetery. Then Jeff explained, "I just need some money to get back to Purdue. I made it to the cemetery and put my last couple of bucks in the tank to get home. I ran over two cents and that darn girl at the gas station made me go out and search my car for two pennies."

    By that time I had come downstairs and Tom and I insisted, "First of all, Jeff, you should never have come home at this hour down the highway with no gas. Go upstairs to bed now and you can go back first thing in the morning." He argued, saying he didn't have any clean clothes to wear, but we told him he could find *something* in his closet. We convinced him, and he slept late the next morning and hung around the house till noon before heading back. We were just so shocked when he came home like that. He had a lot of feelings that he didn't show. It was obvious he missed his sister.

# 39

# Tom

    Jeff had always liked to tinker with things, taking them apart and putting them back together. He had a skate board where he was always checking out the ball bearings, and he dismantled his bicycle as well. If I had hindsight at the time, I would have said, "Well, he's going to be an engineer." I figured he would be good at engineering technology, and that's what he decided on in the end. That field has more hands-on work, whereas a regular engineer does the lay-out work. He took all the necessary courses in high school to prepare himself too. He was always good in math, and he was so good in his computer courses that he ended up testing out of Computers 101. The professor, in fact, had wanted him to be an aide in the class to help other students along, but Jeff worried about keeping his grades up and didn't want to be sidetracked. He didn't want anything affecting his GPA!

*No Words*

Jeff, Freshman at Purdue

He also had decided to go to Purdue. Most kids would pick two or three colleges and send out their applications, hoping to get into one of them. Well, Jeff sent his application to Purdue, and that was it. He had also decided to attend the main campus in Lafayette. He was ready for campus life, and I had told him once or twice that it might be better for him to live on campus and get away. Jill had been more of a homebody, but she was working too at the time, and she probably thought it was just easier to stay at home. After Jill, though, Janet and I had decided that working and going to school wasn't a good thing. It adds too much pressure and they can't concentrate as much on their classes. And yes, I can just picture Jill saying, "Right! You made me work, but you didn't make him work!" If I had to do it all over again I wouldn't let her work either.

I don't feel he had any major problems making the transition from high school to college. Like most other people, he wasn't a straight-A student. He got a couple of bad grades but never seemed to worry about them because he knew he could make them up on the next tests. He held his own and wasn't going to be deterred from what he wanted to do. He was actually working on two degrees at the same time. Engineering Technology was a four-year degree, and he was also going for an associate's degree in computers.

I don't think he was homesick once he arrived on campus and got into the swing of things. Oh, we're all homesick at one time or another, but I think he knew what he was doing and he liked the field he had chosen. As time went on, I was happy he had decided to live on campus because of the social contacts and activities. When you live at home you miss those things. You grow up a little more when you move away. You're on your own and you either make it, or you don't. At home there are more distractions too. Even though you have parties to deal with on campus, at home the whole environment distracts you – your friends, your family. Besides, he could always jump in the car and drive home if he wanted to.

I was just so proud of him. He had set his goals and was accomplishing those goals. It never mattered to me what field he chose or what college he applied to, as long as he went! He was my son, and he was already doing more than I had ever done. We always want our kids to do more than we do, don't we? Experience life more and have greater success. I was proud of both of my kids. They knew what they wanted, and they set about doing it.

There wasn't a day that went by that I didn't think of Jill and miss her. We would go to the cemetery routinely to make sure the grave was in good shape, and of course I would take her flowers. The first holidays without her were rough. Every time our families would get together, they would always have their kids around them. We had Jeff, but Jill wasn't there. She was missed by everyone. She had been so full of fun and so outgoing! She was the life of the party and the light in my heart. At some point someone would always mention Jill, just to incorporate her in the group or break the ice – that's what everyone was thinking about anyway. Whenever we would say a prayer, we would always include Jill. It was reassuring to get together with the family, but it was bittersweet too. I never felt that I didn't want to participate in holidays or celebrations, though. I wasn't going to let anything stop me from doing that, and Jeff needed that normalcy. Life had to move on.

# 40

# Janet

    The college years were definitely the best years of Jeff's life. He got the most out of the whole experience – scholastically, socially – he really came into his own. After his freshman year was completed, he came home that summer and worked at the Parks Department again, for the last time. After that year our lives began changing dramatically.

    One of the first big changes was Tom's retirement from the steel mill in August of 1996. His plant was closing so he was being forced out, but I think after Jill's accident, retirement was welcomed. I really needed him at home more and with shift work that hadn't been possible. At home he was able to give me just a little more emotional support, and I needed that. Even though Jill had been gone two years, our lives were still shaken. So we were happy about the retirement, even though financially it wasn't advantageous because Tom was only fifty-two-years-old.

    At first, Tom didn't do much. He would have been content to sit home and watch TV all day, but I knew he was too young for that. His mind was too young. So I pushed him out the door. Thank goodness he had me, right? He shopped around for a job, hoping for something like thirty hours a week perhaps at a home improvement store of some kind. He had always liked to tinker and he would have excelled at advising people on their projects, but somehow that didn't work out for him. He eventually landed a job with a temporary agency which sent him to work at a factory that made tractor parts. It was a slave shop! Although he was exhausted when he came home, he stuck with it for about nine months.

    Jeff, in the meantime, had started his sophomore year at college. He had never been interested in fraternities but one of his

*No Words*

close friends already belonged to one and kept trying to get Jeff involved. It surprised me when he did decide to join Phi Kappa Theta, but that was the best thing he could have done. Now, he had all those brothers around him whereas before he had no one because he had lost Jill. In the fraternity there was always someone to joke with and horse around with and beat on! He loved that life; it definitely brought him out socially. He was doing things that I never thought he would - like Breakfast Club. In Breakfast Club the boys dressed in weird get-ups before the football games. One time they bought suits from the '50s or '60s at the Salvation Army, and Jeff ended up with a pea green jacket. I couldn't believe it! Typical college antics.

    Gone was the Jeff who never had much to say and just hung out and watched TV. He loved the idea of the brotherhood; he loved the family-type setting. Luckily all of the boys in the group were family-oriented. I'm sure they swallowed the fish and did all the things the other fraternities did, but they were good boys. In fact the last year one of the boys was talking about getting an apartment outside of the big house and wanted Jeff to room with him. Jeff declined and said he would stay put.

    When he started coming back home after he had joined the fraternity, Tom and I could really see the difference. Everyone could, really. He was more social and outgoing. Before when people would say hello to him, he would just give a quick nod. Now, he really shined.

    One of Jeff's friends from school, John, had told him about an internship program with General Electric. It was a work/study program and the interns would spend one semester on campus and the next semester at the General Electric appliance plant in Louisville, Kentucky. John introduced Jeff to the General Electric representative, and both of them were accepted into the program. John was quite a bit older than the other boys at Purdue because he had already gone through mechanics school and then chose to go back and get an engineering degree. He bonded well with Jeff, though, and really took him under his wing. John liked to tease Jeff because Tom and I always moved him. We moved him to

West Lafayette, we moved him to Louisville, and so on. John would say, "You know Jeff, my parents don't do that for me."

"But John, you're an old man!" Jeff retorted. "You're not a kid like me!"

Jeff wasn't homesick in Louisville – he loved it! He loved the apartments they were housed in. He roomed with three other guys - two were from Purdue and the other was from the University of Iowa. They were furnished apartments and very nice. They also had a pool, a volleyball court – just like a country club. He also loved working for GE. He would always be on different shifts, right there on the line with the men. I asked, "Gee Jeff, you want to work shift work for the rest of your life like Dad did?" He told me he liked working with the men and solving problems as they came up. He wasn't somebody who could sit in the office for eight hours. His idea of a good job was hands-on.

It was very different for Tom and me having Jeff in Louisville as compared to Lafayette. I missed him and wished he was closer. We couldn't pop down there for dinner - it was a six-hour drive! We would try our best to go down there for a weekend every once in a while, and he would come home too depending on the weather. He got into the habit of calling me at work. He would be on the line saying, "Hey! What are you doing?" He would talk and talk, never saying much of anything.

At the end of the conversation I would always tell him, "I love you!"

He would always chastise, "Now mother, you don't say things like that on a business phone." What was he doing calling me in the first place, then? Selling me appliances?

So I would end up saying something like, "You know," instead of, "I love you." I guess it was supposed to be a secret.

Even before Jill's accident we had been looking for a new house. Our neighborhood and our town in general were getting much busier and more populated. We knew if we didn't make a change then, we would be putting ourselves in an age bracket where we couldn't afford to make a move. It was then or never.

Since our doctors and my sister Betty lived in Valparaiso, we started looking in that area.

Jeff had told us that moving to a new house was entirely up to us since he was away at college and then off getting a job after that. To him it didn't matter either way. He didn't participate in the planning for the new house and he may have visited it once or twice during construction, but that was about it.

So our lives were indeed changing and progressing. It was still very hard without Jill, and that hasn't changed to this day. It was still difficult to start the day without her, think about her throughout the day, and go to bed at night still missing her. We put memorials in the paper for her birthday or the anniversary of her death, and my brother and sister contributed things on their own, too. Holidays were particularly hard. Because we had Jeff, we still participated with the same kind of flow. Our goal was to make sure his life was as normal as possible. So we celebrated, even though that wasn't what we necessarily felt like doing.

At least once a year, Tom and I met with the parents of the two other girls who had died with Jill. The first year we arranged to meet at Christmas and decorate the little pear tree the nursing school had planted on their grounds in remembrance of our girls. Then we went to lunch and one of the mothers brought angels for all of us. After that, we usually met in February around the time of the accident. We would have dinner or lunch and talk about what had happened in our lives since our last meeting. I felt that we were all dealing with our continuing grief in about the same way. We didn't sit and cry at the dinner table or dwell on the accident or the loss of our girls; we merely talked as friends who had something in common, something that bonded us together. Those meetings lasted for just a few years and then faded. Occasionally, I would get a card or note from one of the parents, usually in February and sometimes on the holidays.

People often suggested trying a support group for parents who had lost children. We never did that. I don't know how to explain it, I simply didn't want to sit there and wallow in my grief. I couldn't deal with it in concentrated doses. I suppose we could have gone just to meet people and say hello and converse for a while, but I couldn't eat and sleep grief all the time. We needed a break.

Because Jeff didn't want to explain about the loss of his sister to his college friends, the boys down in Louisville thought he was an only child. We didn't realize that at first, but later Jeff told us that when they first got to Louisville to start their internship all the boys had to stand up and tell about their families. He said he just wasn't ready to talk about Jill so he told them he was an only child. Well, Tom and I knew he was going to have a rough time being in Louisville when the third anniversary of Jill's death came around. That year the anniversary was on a Tuesday so Tom and I traveled down there the weekend before to spend time with him. We knew he would realize why we were there; we wouldn't have to discuss it in detail. While we were there, Tom pulled aside Jeff's friend John and explained to him about Jill. "If Jeff's a little off-beat come February 24, you'll know why and understand." I'm sure after that there were many that knew about Jill.

I became very protective toward Jeff after losing Jill. One time when he was down in Louisville I woke up in the middle of the night and couldn't sleep. I waited until about 5:30 AM and then told Tom to go call Jeff. "The guys should be getting up for work now, so go call." I wouldn't stop until he did. My son, who slept like a rock, didn't even hear the phone, but we succeeded in waking up his roommates.

They put Jeff on the phone and Tom said, "Is everything okay, Jeff?"

He answered sleepily, "Yes, everything is fine." A couple of days later Jeff instructed me, "Mom, the guys would appreciate it if you didn't call at that hour of the morning." At least I had been relieved. There had been nothing to worry about after all.

# 41

# Tom

After thirty-three years of working shift work at the steel mill, I retired. It wasn't my choice to retire at that time, however. The mill closed down our division, so it was their choice. Even though they had talked about shutting us down for a long time, I wasn't really expecting it. You know the possibility is there, but you're still surprised when it hits you in the face, and I always thought if they did shut us down I would just get transferred to another department. The way it turned out, the only job I could transfer to was that of a laborer, and I couldn't see myself doing that at age fifty-two. Besides, I was going to make just as much monthly income with my pension as I would as a laborer. It wouldn't have made sense to stay.

It was wonderful to be done with the shift work. After thirty-three years I could finally get to see how the other half lived! I was a normal person. I got up in the morning, stayed awake all day, and slept all night!

I figured I would get a part-time job doing something. In fact I knew I would because Janet wasn't about to let me sit around! I would have liked to sit around! I deserved it after thirty-three years of shift work, right? Not according to Janet. I applied at a lumber yard and some home improvement stores, but for some reason they never called me. There's my luck again. Finally, in June of 1997, almost ten months after retiring, I got a position as a factory parts inspector through a temporary agency. It was a hard job and very fast-paced. They would deliver one pallet of parts for me to inspect – they had exact specifications for each of their parts – and as soon as I got done with that pallet they would bring another. Part after part – it was a never-ending battle. It was forty hours a week too, which I wasn't crazy about. The job was supposed to last only six months, though, so I stuck it out. I actually ended up working about nine months in all before I finally quit, and when I did leave the boss begged me to stay, even offering me more money. He said if I ever wanted to come back I would always have a job there. It was nice to be wanted, but my knees couldn't take it anymore. I was on my feet all day.

I don't think Janet and I underwent any major adjustments after my retirement. She told me I had to do all the cooking, but I told her I wasn't a cook. I cleaned once in a while and in general made an effort to help out more. I became Mr. Mom - Janet might disagree with that one - in between golfing and other such important jobs, that is. The major advantage was that Janet didn't have to be alone anymore in the night. She would tell everyone that didn't bother her anymore. Yeah, right.

In the meantime, Jeff was doing well at Purdue and also became involved with the co-op internship program. I personally thought that was a great opportunity because it gave him hands-on experience. When you graduate from college, especially in a competitive field like engineering technology, you have all these others who graduate right along with you. You apply for a job and there may be ten guys in the room who have the same degree. Who are they going to pick - the one with the highest grades? Or the one who's sitting there with three or four years experience with a good company? Well, of course they'd pick the one with experience. You can't beat it.

His co-op experience was at General Electric down in Louisville. He oversaw a specific line, and on his line they made dishwashers. He was like the line foreman, or at least the trainee foreman, and had definite responsibilities like any other supervisor. He ensured the lines kept up with schedules, went to job meetings, and worked on assigned projects to improve the lines. Unfortunately, I never got to see the plant he worked at or what he did on a day-to-day basis. I would really have liked that. One semester the regular foreman became ill and Jeff had to take on additional responsibility. I thought it was amazing they trusted him with that, but he was that good! He really took it to heart.

He started with the co-op in his second year at Purdue and alternated semesters with campus work after that. Normally, the students only do four semesters of co-op but Jeff had already decided to do an extra semester, making five total. His bosses wanted to hire him after graduation and started talking to him about that early on. He loved the Louisville area as well so I figured things would work perfectly.

Once I retired I felt I was able to become more involved in Jeff's life, even though he was in college by that time. Janet and I could at least drive down to Lafayette on the weekends and go to games with him and participate in other activities. He came home for weekends too, at least the semesters when he was in Lafayette. I would always warn him, "Now Jeff, you have to be careful. Make sure you don't drive crazy." Of course, kids do that anyway. You can't stop them from being who they are, and he liked his fast cars. One time we had a conversation about driving down to school and I asked him what his fastest time was. (It took me about an hour and twenty minutes.)

He said, "Oh, I made it there in about an hour."

"You must have been traveling pretty fast!" I told him.

He just grinned and said, "Yeah Dad, but Jill made it in forty-five minutes in the Camaro."

We had been talking about getting a new house for over ten years. We liked where we were at, but with our lives changing and Jill's death, it made it different somehow. I don't think we were recovering much from Jill's loss by staying there; it was too obvious she was missing. I just think it was time for a change. You reach that point where you *have* to do something different. That's where I was. I felt like I had to get out – go somewhere else.

We looked around at several areas but found we liked the Valparaiso area best. Janet picked out a corner lot – her favorite - in a newer subdivision. I had no problem with that subdivision because they had a golf course right on site. Also, the neighbor who lived next door to us at the old house bought the lot across the street from the new house – just by coincidence! We decided to build rather than buy an existing house because I had precise specifications. At first we didn't know what we wanted, other than we knew it had to be bigger than what we had currently. The old one was only 1500 square feet, and we figured Jeff would want to bring his friends home on weekends, and eventually he would get married and we'd have grandkids running around. We'd need the extra space! So I began sketching ideas.

We looked all over but couldn't find any plans we liked. Finally, we decided on a builder and he referred me to an architect, and together he and I designed the house. The front is a two-story but the back is a story-and-a-half. Many people say they've seen this house here or there, but that can't be true. There were no floor plans before we drew them up.

This time I wasn't doing any of the work in building the house. I guess I was just tired and I wanted it turn-key. I planned to move in and then go play golf. I left myself one project, though. The bonus room is unfinished, if I ever get ambitious. I do small things here and there, but nothing extraordinary.

The building started in August of 1997 and moved along at a rapid pace. The builder was doing a good job, too, and we had no complaints. We ended up with 2160 square feet, almost a house-and-a-half from what we had. Our goal was to be in before Christmas, and on December 17 the moving truck arrived.

# 42

# Janet

Moving out of the old house wasn't as hard as I thought it would be, perhaps because it hadn't yet sold. We actually ended up leaving a few things behind, including a twin bed, the microwave, a coffee cup, and even a car in the garage! At the time Tom was still working at the parts factory so he would drop me off at the old house every morning around 6:00 AM, I would lie down for a while, then later get up and take the car out of the garage and drive to work. After work I would drive back to the old house, park the car in the garage, and Tom would pick me up on his way home. Sometimes the old house felt kind of eerie with most of the furniture gone. It was just an empty house now – not a home. So when it eventually sold, it wasn't difficult to finally walk away.

We had packed over a period of several months, mostly because there was so much to move. It amazed me how much we had accumulated over the years! My sister had done the packing in Jill's room while I worked in a different room, as she knew it would be hard. We brought everything that was in her room. I never could sell any of her belongings and only gave things away if people requested specific items.

We scheduled moving day so it was close to the time Jeff was home for Christmas break, and overall the transition was amazingly easy. I was excited about the new house, and we were living closer to my family – my brother, my sister, and even Diane. Even Jeff loved his new, bigger bedroom. He graduated to a double bed rather than his old twin mattress. I had offered to buy him a whole new bedroom set, in fact, but he wasn't interested. As long as he was comfortable watching TV and playing his video games, he never minded what the furniture looked like!

Really the biggest adjustment I had to make came after we sold the old house. It now took me much longer to get to work rather than the usual five minutes! It made for a long day because the old house was so close I could go home for lunch, maybe start dinner or do a load of laundry, or just kick back if I was tired. Now I was leaving at 8:00 AM and not returning till 5:00 PM. You're probably thinking, "Well, that's normal!" But it wasn't normal for me! I missed the convenience of being so close to home, but eventually I grew to love the drive, especially in the spring or summer. I took different back roads and "browsed."

1998 began and Jeff was still doing very well in school. He loved his work, he loved his buddies, and rarely did he express any ongoing grief about Jill's loss - until his twenty-first birthday, that is. He called from Lafayette early that evening. He was sobbing into the phone and the despondency was clear in his voice. "Mom, here I am," he cried. "Jill wasn't at my graduation, and she's not here on my twenty-first birthday." He wept on and on.

My heart was breaking to hear him in so much despair, and I assured him, "Dad and I are going to get in the car and we'll be right down."

He started to calm down and told us, "No, no, no, that's alright." So I phoned my niece Karen, who was also at Purdue. She went right over to Jeff along with her boyfriend and took him out for the evening. Later, all he would say was that it was the lousiest birthday he ever celebrated.

Tom and I didn't discuss much about our grief. It had been four years since Jill's passing but even so the ache and emptiness still flowed right beneath the surface. We were functioning. At times I might look at Tom while he was working in the yard or sitting in the living room and notice he was crying. Other times, I would be driving in the car or doing something around the house and start crying too. That became a part of life.

One day my sister suggested a local therapist who was supposed to be excellent "in case I wanted to make an appointment." I think she felt I wasn't accepting Jill's death as well as I could, even though I was functioning in everyday life. I certainly didn't feel I was clinically depressed or withdrawn or anything like that. I was emotional, sure, every now and then. Yet when she told me about him I took it seriously. I had always wished for someone I could talk to about my hang-ups, like my sometimes irrational fears. I needed someone knowledgeable who could help me sift through the multiple issues that concerned me, not just grief. So I made the appointment – thought I would give it a run. Tom went along with me. I was supposed to go alone, but I asked the therapist if he minded if Tom sat in. He said no, so there we were. We talked about different things but he seemed to zero in on my grief. After the very first time I saw him, I felt that it wasn't going to be productive. I knew I was there mainly because it was my sister's suggestion, not because I was plagued by a nest full of irritating problems. I don't believe people can begin to realize the depths of another person's mind, soul, memories, or experiences. There was so much I would have liked unraveled, but for some reason, I didn't think he was going to get me where I wanted to go. Thinking perhaps I was giving up too soon, I made one more appointment.

    I hadn't had any anxiety attacks, like I had after Larry's death, for a long time. In the years that followed Larry's death, in fact, I only had maybe half a dozen. It surprised me after what I went through in losing Jill and then my mother that I hadn't had one continuous attack! I don't understand how, but I was able to function through all of that. Oh there were times when I didn't want to get out of bed, but I would say to myself, "No, you *have* to do this." I had read a couple of books that explained how people can get to the point where they don't even go outside, and I thought, "No, that's not going to happen to me. I am going to go out, and I'm not going to get dizzy, and I'm going to be alright, just get up and go." So most of the time I talked myself through my anxieties. Then I would go for a long time and not have a problem. Or rather than get dizzy, I would get nervous and the adrenalin would start pumping, and of course fear blows everything out of proportion. I had some medication to take whenever I really needed it.

After the occasional anxiety bouts would subside, I would always feel I was on shaky ground for a while. To me, it felt like I was wired. It's like when somebody scares you and you jump, you're on edge for a time afterwards. I had to focus and labor to calm my nerves.

In January of 1999 I had my worst attack ever. I have no idea what triggered it, but before they had always been something I could handle - I could still function in spite of the fears and feelings of panic. But that one was different. I remember I had just gotten out of the shower and was thinking I needed to get dressed to go to my aunt's. I was toweling off when the dizziness hit. I hate that sensation of dizziness; it robs you of control. If I had been a person who wasn't always afraid maybe I could have blown it off, but immediately my nerves swelled and I felt faint. I lay down and couldn't even lift my head, it was swirling so fast. That attack lasted the longest, and I was off work for a few days. I needed that long just to get back under control. Tom, once again, was very supportive. Trying his best to relax me, he kept me in bed with cool compresses on my head.

After a week or so I was back to functioning again as usual. Life was moving along. Jeff was down in Louisville that semester. He was now a junior in college and this was his last rotation as an intern. Up until that time he had not had many romantic interests but lately he had been talking to a pharmacy student at Purdue who he had met through a friend. He had actually been putting in some long hours talking to her and ended up inviting her to a formal fraternity dance. He even splurged for a new suit! He had his whole life in front of him, and our goal was to help make that life as wonderful as possible.

# 43

# Tom

We lived in our first house for twenty-seven years, from 1970 to December 1997. That was a long time, and I was actually kind of sad to leave it. Of course I was enthused about the new house, there were just so many memories we were leaving behind. Jill's bedroom had stayed the same until we boxed everything up in the moving process. That was the most difficult part of the move, I think. It felt like we were packing away a part of our lives; there was so much yearning for life as it once was. It wasn't a final goodbye, though, because we basically ended up moving her room from the old house to the new. We have one bedroom upstairs that we began referring to as "Jill's room," mainly because it's her furniture in it – even the pictures on the wall. It makes it easier, because to me it *is* Jill. Besides, it's more convenient to talk about a room if you've got it designated! Even Janet sometimes calls it, "Jill's room."

We moved in time for Christmas, which was pleasant – not exciting. We decorated a little but the sadness of Jill's loss carried over, and perhaps part of me thought it might lessen because we were away from the old house. I didn't expect to forget it altogether, maybe just ease it a bit. It didn't. Still, Jeff was home and we were a family.

That spring I quit my job as a parts inspector, but it wasn't long until I found another job, the one I still work today. The subdivision where we now live has a golf course, and in April 1998 I began there as a starter ranger. That's where you work with the pro shop – I stood by the first tee and kept track of the people who were teeing off and the times. It was my job to keep everything organized and running smoothly without back-ups. I inquired there because I wanted to play golf too and working there

I could play for free! It's like belonging to a country club and not having to pay! That was about the first time anything ever worked out so smoothly for me. It's seasonal, though. I work from April till the middle of November, five days a week but just part-time. After two years I transferred over to the maintenance department, which is where I work now. I enjoy the work, but like any other job it has its good points and its bad. Most people think, "Wow! It must be great to work out on a golf course and be out in the open enjoying the weather!" But some days it's downright sweltering, some days it's raining, there are bugs and bees, some days it's cold... It's not all peaches. One time I accidentally ran over a beehive and got stung three times in the neck!

Janet had often told me I never talked to her enough. That surprised me as I thought we always said what needed to be said. One day her sister mentioned a certain therapist and Janet decided we should try that, so we made an appointment. He asked a lot of questions on our first visit – just normal questions that anyone else would ask. He was trying to get to know us I suppose. I remember when we left, we really didn't feel like we had accomplished much. He knew more about us, yes, but *we* didn't know more about us. A few times Janet asked him specific questions, and he answered with something that wasn't really applicable to our situation. We ended up making another appointment, I suppose just to give him the benefit of the doubt!

A few people suggested we go to a grief support group as well, but we never wanted to do that. I felt those groups were probably fine for people who couldn't really deal with losing a child or couldn't talk about it without getting distraught, but we were always able to talk about Jill even though it was very painful at times. At least that was my opinion; perhaps Janet looked at it differently. I felt that as long as we had each other, we could get through anything. It had been five years since Jill's death and we had survived. What could possibly happen that could be as bad as that?

# 44

# Tom and Janet

*(Author's note: Tom's words are in italics, Janet's are in regular script.)*

The phone rang about 7:00 PM on February 4, 1999. I got up to answer it; Janet was just relaxing in front of the TV. "Hello Mr. Rosko?" It was a man's voice I couldn't identify. "This is Jeff's boss at General Electric down in Louisville. I just wanted you to know how sorry I am and ask if there is anything at all I can do for you."

I felt a cold wave ripple through me, and I replied rather puzzled, "You're sorry about what?" Already my throat was starting to tighten and a deep burning began in my temples and spread downward over my body. I was scared. I knew something was terribly wrong.

"You mean you don't know?" I heard him say as if from a great distance.

"No, I don't know. Know what?" I was fishing for information – trying to get him to tell me what the problem was.

"I'm so sorry – I thought enough time went by that you would have been notified," he stammered as though he were in pain. He kept apologizing, and my fear started to choke me. It was the phone call about Jill all over again. They refused to tell me she was dead over the phone, but I knew in my mind if it was that bad, she had to be dead. That was the worst I could imagine, and when he kept saying how sorry he was, I knew Jeff was gone now too.

"Do I need to come down there?" I asked him. I wanted confirmation before my fear overcame me. I was working in the hypothetical, assuming what had happened. Maybe I was wrong. The tears were stinging my eyes.

*"No, no, you needn't come. Jeff's been killed. He was standing in a video store. A van plunged through the window and killed him. I'm so sorry. The van ran over him. It happened around 3 or 4:00 PM. I thought you would have known by now. I'm so sorry."* My fear evaporated and I felt utterly lost. There was nothing I could do. I couldn't save him, I couldn't go to him. He was gone. Gone. I turned to look at Janet. I could tell by the look of thick pain and disbelief in her eyes that she knew even without me speaking the words.

I didn't want to hear what Tom was saying on the phone. "What do you mean you're sorry? Do I need to come down there?" I didn't want to hear that overwhelming sadness in his voice; I didn't want to see his body shudder. I had seen and heard it before and I knew what it all meant. It couldn't be happening again. I couldn't believe it. "But look at Tom," I told myself. "It is happening." Another nightmare and we would never awaken.

*He told me the few details he knew about the accident – just enough to satisfy me at the time. I didn't want to hear what he had to say, but I knew I had to listen. I tried to regain enough composure to focus on the practical. Now what did I need to do? The part of my mind that was still rationale was trying to pull it together.*

I got on my cell phone and called my sister. "Jeff's been killed. He's dead. It's happening all over again." In what seemed like an instant she and my brother-in-law Bob were at our house. No one could believe this was happening. We were trying to think of who we could call to confirm everything, but finally Bob convinced us to wait for the police to come. That was really all we could do. So we kept pacing, anxiously waiting for what we knew would come.

The officer came around 8:00 PM. He was solemn yet kind and simply said he had some very bad news. Tom told him we already knew. He apologized that it had taken so long for us to be notified but their computer system was down and he hadn't known our name or address. He had come as soon as he could.

*He didn't really know the details of the accident, but he gave me the number of the officer in Louisville to call. He stayed for a while and even asked if Janet needed a doctor or if there was anything else he could do, but he couldn't do anything. What could he do?*

*I immediately called the Louisville police and talked to the sergeant, who gave me a good rundown of what happened at the accident. Jeff and his friend Rob were in a video store. A nine-year-old girl and her mother were also in the store, and the girl had asked to go sit in their minivan. She was wearing a prosthesis on her hand and told her mother it was bothering her and she wanted to take it off. Her mother gave her the keys, and she started the van to listen to the radio. She placed the van in reverse, causing it to roll backward and strike a small tree. She then put the van in forward, crashing it through the front window of the store and covering 60 feet before finally coming to rest against the store's rear wall. Although both Jeff and Rob were hit by the van, Rob had gone over the top of the van whereas Jeff had been thrown underneath. Rob suffered head and leg injuries, and apparently Jeff died of head injuries from hitting the ground upon impact. It all sounded so surreal, and still the only fact I was struggling to grasp was that Jeff was dead.*

*After we had final confirmation, I called my brothers Jerry and Don and also my cousin Mickey down in Florida to go tell my parents – again. My aunt picked up the phone when I called and right away she gave the phone over to Mickey. I'm sure she could tell how distraught I was and she didn't want to hear what I had to say. I gave Mickey enough time to get over to my parent's house and tell them, and then I called there myself. Janet and I had been concerned for their health when we lost Jill, and now here it was, the same thing again five years later with Jeff and thirty-eight years after losing their own son, Butch. We knew it would hit them hard.*

I called Diane and my brother. Everyone wanted to know if they should come over but we told them no, it was too late. I called my boss to let her know I wouldn't be in the next day. They were all in such disbelief. If someone would call you on the phone, God forbid, and tell you your child's been killed – that's just so hard to comprehend. Especially the second time around. We never wanted to pick up the phone again.

I watched Tom. He was numb and in shock. He wandered from room to room.

*You can't sit, you can't walk. There's nothing to say that doesn't catch in your throat. Fragments run through your mind but don't compute. I was helpless. Jeff was in Louisville dead and I was here. There was nothing I could do.*

Betty stayed overnight. Tom went to bed to try and get some sleep, Betty slept on the couch, and I sat up on the loveseat in the living room. I sat there all night and was very quiet. I didn't want to disturb Betty. I thought back just two weeks before to the worst anxiety attack I had ever had. Had that been a premonition? Here I was still encouraging myself and trying to bring myself out of it, reassuring myself that everything was going to be okay. I was getting back on the road again, overcoming the fears that always threatened to control my life. I sat there and held the tears behind the gate of emotion I was feeling, and the numbness that took over allowed that gate to stay closed. How could this happen again? Where did we go wrong? I immediately thought, "What could I ever have done to deserve this?" Whatever faith I had left just evaporated at that moment. I hoped I could make it through the next few days without collapsing. I had to be there for Jeff; I had to be with him. Thoughts raged through my mind like bolts of electricity.

*It was just so unfathomable. What is the chance of lightening striking in the same place twice? What are the odds of both our children getting killed like that?*

## No Words

Jeff's accident had been so bizarre. If he had been out drinking or partying – even if he had stepped off the curb before the stoplight changed, it would have made more sense, but to be standing in a video store and having a nine-year-old girl crash a minivan through the window and kill him? It really was like being struck by lightening.

*There was no real anger. I was lost and numb. I felt a deep and absolute sorrow – for Jeff, for Jill, for us, and each other. They both had worked so hard to get where they were. If there was any anger, that's where it lay. God never let them finish what they started.*

*I slept on and off that night. I thought only of the moment, I couldn't look ahead even to the next few days. You know, Janet and I had been talking about getting back into the church and going regularly again. Then bang! Jeff is taken from us. It was like someone saying, "Hey, you don't belong in church!" That's what I felt. We got hit again, but this time there were no children left.*

# 45

# Tom and Janet

*(Author's note: Tom's words are in italics, Janet's are in regular script.)*

Jeff died on a Thursday, just like Jill. Friday morning visits and phone calls from family and friends started early. Irene, a lady I worked with who years before had lost her husband and then six months later lost her daughter, stopped by with a box of donuts and told us how sorry she was. Both the local and Louisville newspapers started calling, wanting pictures and a story. Tom talked to one reporter locally who actually wrote a very nice story. It told a little about Jeff and his life as well as the details of the accident. Even radio stations were calling us. Some picked up on the fact that we had lost both children.

*We called Father Jerry that morning. He came over and we sat at the kitchen table and said a prayer. He asked Janet and me to each say something about Jeff. I told him I didn't think I'd be able to get through that, and I didn't. I just couldn't. I was back on that roller coaster of emotions, and as we sat there they all just boiled to the surface.*

A few neighbors also came over and brought food. We called Rendina's Funeral Home the night before and had expected them to go down and pick up Jeff's body, but they decided it would be better to fly him home rather than fight February weather. That was Jeff's first plane ride. I often thought later I should have flown down there to come home with him so he wouldn't be alone.

*We also spoke to the coroner in Louisville, who informed us he would have to perform an autopsy because of the circumstances of the accident. We didn't like that, but no one gave us a choice. Rendina's had to wait until after the coroner was done with him to bring him home.*

My brother and sister came by around noon to take Tom and me to the funeral home to begin arrangements. We wanted a blue casket just like Jill's was pink. They were the same caskets – both equal - no problems in heaven! We wrote the obituary. Rendina's were just as helpful to us this time as they had been with Jill. We couldn't have had more support.

Afterwards, we went to select flowers. I told them I wanted masculine colors – no pinks or anything like that. Then we came home. One of our friends was cleaning up the kitchen and getting things organized around the house. My sister-in-law Patti was taking phone messages – there were so many. Neighbors were still coming over; those we didn't even know were bringing food trays. None of them wanted to come in. One neighbor who had lost a child previously brought over a cake, but that was difficult for her. That pain just never goes away. She had told another neighbor she couldn't imagine going through it twice. Even through our numbness we felt overwhelming support, just as we had with Jill. Sometimes it came from different people, but the support was still there.

Later, my niece came over and I mentioned to her that Jeff liked Garth Brooks. I asked her if there were any of his songs that would be appropriate for the funeral, and she suggested *The River*. She let me listen to it on tape and we ended up requesting it for the funeral. We weren't sure Father Jerry would allow it, many priests probably wouldn't. There were some songs we wanted for Jill that they wouldn't play in the church, but Father Jerry said we could play whatever we wanted for Jeff.

We had to call Jeff's roommates down in Louisville and ask them to pick out Jeff's clothes for us. He had just bought that new suit for the dance the week before, and Tom and I had never even seen it. It was hard for us to ask them to do that and I'm sure even more difficult for them, but we had no one else to ask. I told them to imagine they were getting ready for a dance or something similar and pick out the shoes, socks, even the underwear they would wear. Then they had to take it to the coroner's office so it could all be shipped with his body.

My niece spent the second night with us. No one wanted us to be alone this time. If our family had kept close watch on us with Jill, they did even more so with Jeff.

*On Saturday we had a bit of a break – at least from the activity if not from our desolation. The sorrow ravages your soul, yet it was impossible to sit and cry continuously. We were emotionally weary. We were stressed and worn – empty. We hoped for things to take our mind off the deep grief if only for a short time, to pull us back to reality.*

*Janet's brother spent a lot of time Saturday reminiscing about Jeff. "Oh, I remember when Bo did this, or Bo did that." He always called him Bo. I think it helped everyone to reminisce. We were all thinking about him, talking about him in the present tense like he was still there. We knew we were never going to see him alive again, but we knew he was still with us. We felt his presence, we felt both kids.*

*Mostly we were just dealing with the moment. We felt like hiding in the closet, but everything had to happen in due course.*

Tom's brother and his family were with us, and his parents arrived from Florida. For the family members who couldn't come, there were nonstop phone calls.

That night Betty's two boys stayed with us, and Sunday morning Tom and I got up and made them breakfast and got ready for the wake. Betty and Bob came by to drive us to the funeral home. I didn't even know what to wear – I relied on others to tell me.

We got to the funeral home about a half hour before other people started to arrive, and that was the first time we saw Jeff.

My first thought was that he looked so handsome! It didn't look like he was hurt at all.

His hair had always been dark and curly. He kept it so short – whenever it started to grow the curls would start showing. He never wanted anyone to touch his hair either, but I walked up to the casket and kept patting and rubbing his head. I had to feel him, you understand? Mr. Rendina came over to me and asked me not to touch the one side of his head because that's where he was hurt. He asked me to be careful. I just thought he was so handsome and he looked so polished in his new suit.

*Just like at Jill's, quite a lot of people showed up. Many were the same but there were others too because their lives were different. Jeff's whole fraternity showed up, including a 70-year-old fraternity brother who read about Jeff in the paper. The other fraternity brothers were overwhelmed and gathered around him. They felt a bond with him because he was a brother of theirs, despite their age difference.*

When Jeff's friends started arriving, they reached out to shake my hand but I told them no, they had to give me a hug. His friend Jeremy came in and I noticed his necktie. "Hey Jeremy, nice tie," I joked. He laughed too because it was Jeff's tie – a tie that he had never worn and gave to Jeremy when he needed one. He never gave it back because he liked it so much. It was his favorite.

Another man came and introduced himself to us. He didn't know us at all but said he read about the accident in the paper and felt he just had to come.

*There were managers from the General Electric plant in Louisville that came. Also a couple of the workers – just the regular line men – were there. Even the Dean of Nursing from Valparaiso University came and a few other professors who had known Jill.*

I told one of Jeff's roommates from Louisville that if there were any unpaid bills from the apartment just let Tom and I know, and we would pay them. "Oh no," he shook his head. "My dad said not to worry about a thing. We'll take care of the rest of them." We had never met the man, but it was so kind of him to do that.

There were a lot of men – fathers – who walked up to us with tears in their eyes. That really struck me. Jeff's first basketball coach walked up to me and said, "You probably don't remember me."

"But I do remember you," I replied. "You're the best coach Jeff ever had." A lot of people came from Jeff's past and reminisced about when he was little.

*We tried to thank everyone that came. We appreciated it. Because of the line we couldn't talk long, but we did the best we could. I don't think you can expect anything more of a parent, just to be gracious and value the support that's being given at the time.*

Mr. Rendina's wife, Marsha, whom we had known for a long time, came into my view and I approached her to say hello. Shaking her head, she looked at me and put her hand up as if to stop me. "Oh no, I can't talk to you right now. I'm sorry, I just can't talk." She was so upset. She kept walking away, so I let her go. She was keeping herself under control, but she knew if I talked to her that control would be lost. I understood, and I respected her space. Everyone handles grief a little differently. I've learned that.

*That night the fraternity boys had a service for Jeff. That was the first time they had done that so it was very difficult for them. It turned out so very nice. We also had Father Jerry's service.*

Tom's uncle, who had curly hair like Jeff, was probably the last to leave that night. He was talking to me, telling me how sorry he was and to take care of myself, then he turned to go. He stopped suddenly and said, "Oh, my gosh! I have to say goodbye to Jeff!" I was so taken aback by that – nobody had been that open. It caught me off guard, but I thought it was so considerate.

*Everyone was taking it hard, but you never saw it. They were trying to be strong for Janet and I and even each other, I know, but we could see that they were hurting and puzzled. I saw my brother cry. I saw my dad go up and rub Jeff's coat or his hand. If you looked, you could see the anguish and you could feel the heaviness.*

We were exhausted by the time we arrived home from the wake. We went to bed and my nephews again stayed the night. We slept and tried to absorb any peace and energy that might be found.

Around 9:00 AM Monday morning my sister drove us to the funeral home. People started to arrive almost immediately. There were so many! It made us feel good that people cared so much. I remember after everything was over, I was looking through the sign-in book and the first name on the list was the boss who hired me for my first job back in 1964. I didn't even know he had been there, but he came.

*We knew that day was going to be hard. It wasn't as though we wanted to hurry up and get it over with because we knew it was our last day with Jeff. Emotionally we were worn down, but we didn't want it to end.*

*After a small service everyone said their last goodbye to Jeff. Only the immediate family was left. When that final moment arrived, I just didn't want to leave. I felt immobilized. I was a fountain of grief. The Rendina's were nudging us. It was time to go to church, time to close the casket, time to say goodbye to our son.*

We had a full mass at the church – two priests and two deacons. I remember my eyes being hot with tears, but I kept my sobs in check. After the church we went to the mausoleum because of the weather rather than to the gravesite, although Mr. Rendina drove everyone past the gravesite on the way out – just like with Jill.

*Jeff was buried next to Jill. There is one headstone with two separate footstones. We had inscribed a Purdue insignia in one corner, a mustang on another – he loved his Mustangs – then below his name are his Greek letters. We were glad that Jeff had helped pick out the headstone, especially the praying hands. They were what he wanted for his sister.*

Jeff's fraternity brothers were the pallbearers, and they put his fraternity pin on his coat. Rob, the friend who was with him in the video store, was on crutches so my nephew Kevin stood in for him, but Kevin was a Purdue engineering grad too, so that was a good choice.

Afterwards we went to the church hall for a catered dinner. We let all the boys who came from Kentucky go through the line first because they had to drive back. So many of those young men came – so many went to communion for him, with him.

Tom and I were very quiet during the funeral. We knew we just had to make it through the day. If we let our self-preserving wall down just a little bit, it would crumble. He looked after me and I attempted to do the same for him.

I knew Tom was taking Jeff's death even harder than Jill's. Even through today, I think he's had a harder time with losing Jeff.

*I think it's the cumulative effects of losing both of them. The grief from Jill's death has never lessened, and now the heartache of losing Jeff has just been added to it. Losing a daughter is no easier than losing a son.*

*Janet and I were just trying to survive moment by moment. We were going through the motions and riding the waves of* emotions. We could fully understand what was happening but couldn't fathom why it happened. It wasn't until the days progressed and everyone started getting back to normal – and normal wasn't there for us anymore – that we understood the depth of our loss.

# 46

# Tom and Janet

*(Author's note: Tom's words are in italics, Janet's are in regular script.)*

*"Jeff's death was a freak accident."* I can't tell you how it sickens me every time I hear that ridiculous statement. To believe that does grievous injustice to our son and his memory. It mocks any sense of fairness or ethics. It wasn't an accident. Our son had been killed, and someone should have been held accountable.

By the end of the second day after Jeff's death, we had a pretty good understanding of what had transpired at the scene. I had spoken with the police sergeant and the coroner, and each one relayed the same story, though a few more details emerged each time they told it. Later, I also received a copy of the police report which revealed even more.

At about 3:55 in the afternoon of February 4, Jeff and his friend Rob were in a video store in St. Matthews, Kentucky. There were five other customers in the store along with an employee, and two of those customers included a woman with her nine-year-old daughter. The girl had a prosthesis on her right arm that was bothering her so she had asked her mother if she could go to their minivan to remove it. She gave her the keys. The girl started the van to listen to the radio. She then shifted the car into reverse, which she knew how to do, she explained to the police, because her mother had sometimes allowed her to reach over from the passenger seat and shift the van while she was behind the wheel. The van began to roll backwards, striking the curb and a tree in the parking lot median. Three witnesses outside of the store saw the van hit the tree with the girl behind the wheel. One yelled out to her, "Hey! Hey!" The girl then put the van in forward, although she claimed to have no memory of that, and pressed the accelerator "to make the car go back into its parking space." Witnesses attested that the van's motor revved and shifted into high gear, with the vehicle crashing through the front store window. The little girl was seen behind the wheel, although when the van crashed through the building she moved to the passenger side "to get away from the air bag." One of the store's customers ran to the van when it came to a stop at the back of the store, opened the passenger door and pulled the girl from the vehicle. He handed the girl to her mother, who was following close behind. He then turned off the engine, though the horn was still blaring.

Jeff and Rob were the only two customers hit by the van, with Rob thrown up over the van and Jeff forced under. Rob became hysterical when he saw Jeff and cried, "Oh, my God! Oh, my God! I can't believe he's dead!" One of the witnesses who was out in the parking lot at the time was a paramedic. He rushed in, giving first aid to Rob with facial and leg injuries, and eventually transported him to the hospital in his own vehicle. Jeff was face down with his arms at his side, probably never knowing what hit him. The medical examiner's report said he died of a closed-head injury, likely being knocked backward when the van hit and then rolled face down as the van passed over him. When the police arrived, the mother and the girl were found sitting on the floor away from the scene and although upset were able to provide the necessary information.

Before the van crashed through the window, the mother had been standing at the front counter, checking out her video, in full view of the window.

The day after we learned of Jeff's death, we contacted our attorney. We knew there would be paperwork to be taken care of, just as with Jill's death. We also let him know there were unusual circumstances involved with Jeff's death and some other legal matters may need resolved on down the line. He advised us to wait and let the police and prosecuting attorneys do their jobs. We would see what they came up with.

From the first day I didn't quite feel that everything was being investigated and pursued as it should have been. One point *that really disturbed me was that no ticket was issued at the accident. We knew someone was at fault – I mean a nine-year-old girl was driving the vehicle for heaven's sake.*

I did talk to a friend who is an attorney, and she told me that at times when there are questions of possible liability the judge prefers the officer not to issue any tickets until he completes the investigation. They don't want the officer making judgment calls at the scene.

*Nevertheless, we sat back and waited as we had been advised, trusting that justice would prevail. In the meantime, a friend of Jeff's from Louisville recommended a few well-respected local attorneys. We attempted to contact the first on the list but discovered the girl's mother had already hired that firm. So we hired another, and they investigated the liability of the motor company and the video store. They found no fault with either.*

*Finally, on March 26 we received a letter from the prosecuting attorneys stating that "after complete and thorough review" no criminal charges would be pursued. "We are sorry for your loss," blah blah blah.*

*Janet and I contacted our attorney and he suggested we make an appointment to meet with the prosecuting attorneys face to face. Possibly forcing them to see us as people rather than a name and address would cause them to rethink their decision. We certainly made that appointment, but it was a worthless attempt. Their minds were already resolved and they held strong that there was "no prosecutable offense." It appeared they would never conclude unequivocally that the girl had been driving the vehicle. Yes, they agreed she was behind the wheel - but did that mean she was actually driving it? Exasperated, I stammered, "How did she move the van if she wasn't driving it? Do you think it went into gear on its own? This was a newer vehicle – you have to put your foot on the brake to adjust the gear shift. Besides that, there were witnesses who saw her backing up the van and taking it forward!" My frustration was bubbling.*

We fully realized that the mother did not say to the child, "Here are the keys, go start the van and drive it." In the police report, however, the girl explained she knew how to put the car in gear because her mother had taught her. Doesn't this assign responsibility? One attorney also told us that the girl's mother was "close to a nervous breakdown" and under treatment. Well you know what? Our nerves were about shot too.

*I started hammering at them. I had had enough of them telling us no one was responsible. In my mind, the real reason they chose not to pursue the case was because they felt it couldn't be won. It wasn't that laws weren't broken, it's that they couldn't find a jury to convict a nine-year-old girl! They weren't going to waste their time.*

I feel they didn't fight for us because we weren't part of the clan. We would drive home to our own neck of the woods and it would be over. They were taking care of their own. I told the prosecutor that Jeff loved that community. He came down as a student and worked and lived there, paid his taxes, did not disturb the community and in fact was an asset to it. We should have at that point gone straight to the TV station and talked to one of those reporters who kept calling us. They even wanted to bring their news van all the way to Northwest Indiana for an interview. The squeaky wheel gets the grease. We should have known that.

After that meeting Tom and I drove down to the river to a place Jeff had once taken us. We just sat there in our car, thinking. We did call a reporter from a local radio station and told her it had been decided that no charges were to be filed. She wanted to come and interview us, but we said no. At that point neither of us had anything left to give. Besides, we didn't want Jeff's death to become a circus with reporters hounding us. It wouldn't have changed our loss, and I wanted to keep things respectful. That was our son's life.

At the time we didn't feel we had a lot of backing from our friends and relatives. I mean, they weren't telling us to go after them or anything like that, and we knew we ourselves were in deep emotion and not always thinking rationally. Later, we found out that everyone wished we would have pursued it more strongly, including Jeff's co-workers at the Louisville plant.

*Responsibility needed to be accepted. There was a wrong that needed to be accounted for. She may as well have taken a loaded gun and shot him. Even if they had prosecuted the case and lost, that would have been enough. At least the attempt would have been made.*

We never wanted the mother convicted and sent to prison. She had a family to take care of. We just wanted something, even if it were community service and some therapy possibly for the little girl. The question that kept running through my mind was how did she lose her hand? Was it a birth defect? Was it neglect on the parent's part? Was it just a mischievous child? It's the question of the prosthesis, and now that she's got it do Mom and Dad let her do anything she wants because she's handicapped and they feel sorry for her? What's the mentality here? Is someone else going to be hurt if it happens again?

*We should have been thinking more of Jeff than of the consequences to that family – if there were any. Apparently they got away scot-free. We talked to our attorney about a civil trial. He told us to pursue civil suit we would have to go through court and see all the pictures and hear all the testimony, and he didn't think we could handle it at that point. Besides, even if we were awarded $10 million, they couldn't pay it. We didn't want them losing their home. Their insurance company had already paid us what they allowed and that, in fact, was an admission of guilt. They would never have paid if they hadn't been responsible, but they paid what they allowed, not for our loss, and that's two different things.*

## No Words

    We really didn't know anything about that family. We weren't allowed to. They may have gone home and just forgotten about it. You know the father sent a big beautiful bouquet of flowers to the funeral home. Mr. Rendina called us and asked us what we wanted to do with them, possibly send them back, but we told him to put them out with the others. The day of the funeral a woman was gathering petals to use at the final service and went towards that bouquet. Tom's niece went up to her and said, "No, I don't want any of those petals in the basket." Everyone knew where those flowers had come from. They could have been draped in black. The father also sent us a letter saying that he was very sorry but accidents happen. Yeah, Tom and I already knew that.
    One year I did put a memorial for Jeff in the Louisville paper. I wanted people down there to remember him, his co-workers and friends. I suppose I also wanted to take a stab at their justice system.

    *You know we saw a picture that was taken at the video store parking lot. Jeff's truck was parked right next to the island where the tree was planted that she backed into. We were amazed to see it right there. She didn't put a scratch on it.*

    So we live with this injustice done to our son, and to this day I feel like I let Jeff down. Jeff would still be here if the basic problem had been taken care of from the start – if Mom had put her child above a $3 video and gone out to the van with her, taken the prosthesis off, or taken her home. Was that video worth another person's life that she couldn't have taken five minutes?

    *The more time that passes the worse it gets. I keep thinking about it and get more aggravated – it's worse now than it was two years ago or even yesterday. I think about what might have been. That little girl ran over our son, killed him, and she and her mother walked away free. They should have been held accountable, but for nothing to happen at all...*

# 47

# Janet

The depth of loss doesn't really impact you immediately. It takes a while to move from stilted shock to noticing how profoundly your life has been affected. Where energy was continuously funneled into the love and caring and concern and hope for one person, suddenly that center is gone. In the void that remains – well, there's just overwhelming emptiness.

After Jill died, we still had Jeff to be concerned about. We were still parents; that identity and all it entailed was still with us. After Jeff died, we weren't parents anymore. There was only the two of us. Even though Jeff was living at Purdue or down in Louisville and we didn't see him very often, we still had that cord of attachment as all parents do. It doesn't matter if your child is home or hundreds of miles away. You still have that connection. You feel him inside you. Now, there were no more phone calls, no more weekend trips, no future planning, nothing to look forward to really. The final cord was terminally severed. I would never hold or laugh or cry with either of my children again.

Tom and I had already re-established our couple's life together with Jeff being away at school. We fit into that empty-nest category I suppose. In our daily consciousness we didn't think in terms of, "Well, Jeff's not coming home to dinner." He wasn't supposed to, whereas when Jill died, we missed her not coming home every night as usual. That was one difference between their losses, although I can't say it made it any easier.

So our day-to-day routine didn't change much, and it's amazing really how people can continue to function in the midst of crushing devastation. You know, after we lost Jill, a few times I secretly wondered if it would have been easier to have lost Jeff instead, but because my love for both children was just as great, I immediately forced those thoughts away. It's just that Jill had such an open personality and could have talked through her sorrow – and mine – whereas Jeff remained so quiet and locked, and I never wanted to upset him by prying into his grief or expecting him to carry some of mine. I wondered at the time, but after losing both I knew the answer. To lose a child is to lose a child. Nothing makes it easier, and it couldn't have been harder.

With Tom, though, I think losing Jeff was more difficult, though he may not have realized that. When the kids were growing up, he just didn't have the type of contact I had with them on a daily basis, going through all their ups and downs. He was usually home for dinner, but that still didn't allow the connection I had. His role was primarily breadwinner; my role was primarily mother, but after Jill's accident and he had retired, he and Jeff bonded more. What Jill and I had when she passed away Tom had with Jeff for the first time, and when Jeff died Tom lost his best friend as well as his son. With Jill's loss he also had a job to get back to, but with Jeff's death he wouldn't be going back to his summer job for several months. He had more time on his hands to think and sometimes that kind of time isn't a gift.

Tom has been very surprised at how many men were and still are so compassionate to Jeff's loss. It was evident at the funeral and in the months that followed – even today. They are family men or men who have lost their own fathers. He was never used to a man coming up and giving him a hug. For one of our neighbors to come up on the golf course and give him a hug – it was just totally outside his realm. "Men don't hug men," was his mentality. But I think it really touches him every time it happens. He talks about it occasionally. "You know I can't believe that," he'll say. "This man walked up to me and gave me a hug. He asked how I was doing." I think men today have less social barriers in showing their emotions. They cook and change diapers. It brings out their feminine side and raises them to a higher level. They're not just the breadwinner, and their wives usually have a job outside the home as well. They take more of an active role in raising their children, and they go with their emotions and don't feel emasculated because of it. Men from our generation can't always say that.

Our first summer without Jeff passed uneventfully. One day was the same as the next. In what seemed to be just a few weeks, the holidays came around and I began thinking about the last Christmas Jeff had with us. He wanted a big, tall tree in our living room because we have a very tall ceiling, so Tom and I picked out a tree that we *thought* was tall, but when we actually brought it home, it wasn't! That first Christmas without Jeff, Tom and I bought one of those pencil trees, narrow but real tall, in honor of Jeff. We laugh every time we decorate it because Tom and I are so much shorter than Jeff was, and we figure Jeff is probably laughing at our attempts to get this angel on top of a ten-foot tree! We always put a Purdue ornament on the tree for Jeff and a Valparaiso University ball for Jill.

Our families were always good to us and included us in all the family gatherings, and we appreciated that. We all knew it would be difficult each and every time, but they let us know they were there to support us. People would do special things too, like my sister's son came to visit from Chicago and stopped to put a wreath at their gravesites. Tom and I didn't even know until we went out there the next time – we were so surprised!

As the months went by, our neighbors and friends spoke of Jeff and Jill less and less. I didn't feel abandoned by them, however, even though I thought of them both as much as ever. On our street alone there are two families that have endured the loss of a child. Sometimes those are the ones who avoid you the most because they know there's not much they can do to alleviate your emptiness.

Tom and I tried going back to the therapist we had started seeing before Jeff passed away. We had gone to him once before Jeff's accident and then I had to cancel our next appointment because of the funeral. Once we resumed, I could tell right away it wouldn't be worth our efforts. He told us several times he had never dealt with a situation like ours – parents losing two children under these circumstances. He said the loss was unimaginable, and after a while Tom and I felt we were consoling him! Tom and I actually chuckled about the situation a few times when we got in our car to leave his office. He would look at me, and I would look at him, and we just shook our heads. We only went about three or four times in all.

After Jill's death I felt the need to go to the cemetery often. After Jeff's accident, though, it was much more difficult to go and see both of their graves there. I still go, but not as often. My sister-in-law plants both graves now. We divide down the middle of the headstone and plant Jeff's side with more masculine colors rather than the pinks and lavenders of Jill's side. Jeff was always a Kansas City fan so we use red and gold, and of course gold is for Purdue too. The only comfort I have in looking at their graves side by side is in knowing they are together. Jeff doesn't have to grieve for Jill anymore, and Jill has her brother to look after her. I see Jeff's sly grin, I hear Jill's bubbling laugh, and I feel my heart cry out.

# 48

# Tom

It's difficult for me to recall the first few weeks and months after Jeff's death. It was more like reliving a nightmare that still haunts you even after the lights go on. I remember thinking I had been through this already. Why must I do it again? I can't say it was harder or easier the second time. One was as bad as the other – even though it was different. You would think that because I had lived through it before and knew what to expect, it wouldn't be as bad. It was. Actually, in some respects it was worse because now Janet and I had lost both of them, but then it couldn't be any worse, could it?

Even through the initial shock and disbelief of Jeff's death, it hit me that Janet and I didn't have anybody left now, just ourselves. We had been convincing our minds for five years that we only had one child. Now we didn't have any. We went from having a family to half a family to no family at all. To me that meant no future. That's why there's nothing worse than losing your kids, because you lose your own future as well. Not only are there no children, there are no son-in-laws or daughter-in-laws, no grandchildren – you've lost them all. What is there to look forward to except growing old together? That's something, but it's lonely.

Janet and I went through a depression, and I can't imagine anyone that wouldn't. We even attended a few more sessions with the therapist we started with before Jeff's accident. Even he told us he had never dealt with a situation like ours before. We went only a few times, but we felt we were doing better just talking to each other and working it out day by day. Therapy might have benefited by bringing us together to talk about certain specific concerns, whereas at home we would spend most of our time in front of the TV or busy with something else. I got to the point where I could say, "Hi, how are you?" instead of just, "Hi." Maybe I was looking for something else but didn't find it, but in the end I knew our own survival would depend on just the two of us.

My concern for Janet has always been the same – that she doesn't go off the deep end, just as her concern for me has always been I suppose. My energy was spent trying to get our lives back on track. You always worry about what's around that next corner. When Jill died we were so concerned that something would happen to Jeff. We went into a hyper-protective mode. Of course we didn't have control over everything he did, but we always told him to be careful, don't speed when you go back to school, call us when you get there – that whole routine. Now we didn't have that protective focus. Janet and I just watched each other and tried to be more attentive. I felt that's what we needed to do and of course I've always been protective towards Janet anyway.

People wanted to help and be a part of our lives, and we felt that was great, but it didn't take the pain away. No matter how many friends we had, it still hurt. You're crying on the inside and laughter is just a momentary diversion. It may last a minute or an hour, but there's always something that reminds you – jerks you back into that harsh reality. I never felt sorry for myself, thinking that just because my kids are gone I'm going to sit and cry and not let any happiness come into my life. I just took everything day by day and what happened, happened. As the months turned into seasons, I had days when I felt good and would be laughing, and then later I would be driving down the street and just start crying. That's happened many days out on the tractor while I'm working – it's a good thing I'm by myself. It just happens. I'm not sad every minute of the day – nobody is, but those ups and downs creep up on you. It's like having cancer for cancer patients. Some days are not as bad as others. Not a day goes by even now when I don't think of them at least once. I walk into a room and look at their pictures. I turn on the radio and listen to a song they liked. They are still with me, and that's not going to change just because I can't see or hear or touch them.

Janet and I talked about the kids a lot – we still do. We think it's better than just clamming up and not talking about them at all. That would be like denying their existence. We've had times when we sit and just laugh about the antics they used to get into. I still talk to *them*, too, and I know Janet does as well.

As time progressed, though, I think I felt somewhat abandoned by our family and friends. People quit coming around as much as they used to, and we rarely have company now. They call, but calling and coming over and spending time is two different things. A telephone can't take the place of companionship. In the early stage after Jeff's death so many people were near and then gradually they just disappeared. I'm not blaming anybody – people just have very busy lifestyles nowadays. I don't think they even realize it, but consequently we are by ourselves quite a bit and that becomes mundane. Every day is Monday around here.

We have appreciated everything that people have done for us. How could you not appreciate people's kindness? One man I play golf with was telling me about his father who was struck by a car and said how he could understand the pain of losing someone you love. I told him about Jeff and Jill. Ever since, once in a while he'll look at me and say, "You look like you need a hug, Tom." And he hugs me! That's fine, if that's the way he feels. I'm not used to that, though. I got hysterical one day many years ago when Janet's father gave me a kiss before we left on vacation. After that I'd keep my distance from him whenever everyone got "kissy." He'd look over at me and give me his big smile.

My kids were just normal kids. We both heard a lot of stories about them from various people after they died, like how kind they were, the nice things they did for other people – things we had no idea about because they didn't come home and tell us those details. They were both well-liked. I know the General Electric plant in Louisville really had high hopes for Jeff. In fact, the morning of his accident his boss sent a memo to the manager stating that Jeff was the best co-op they ever had. I wish Jeff could have seen that memo, but it made me proud nevertheless.

# 49

# Janet

In reflecting back, there are times when I don't know how we have survived. I suppose we have just clung to our day to day routine. In fact, we've become stuck in that routine like a self-rewinding tape. On occasion I get to the point where I feel accustomed to Jill and Jeff being gone, but then guilt creeps in when I start feeling too adjusted to their loss. Part of me wants to move on to other things, and the other part of me is appalled for even considering it.

I used to think it was the end of the world and there were no tomorrows. I lived for my kids, and my kids were my tomorrows. There were weddings and grandchildren to look forward to. There were vacations and birthdays and holidays to plan. Now we don't have that. The future we had molded so carefully has been erased.

When Tom and I were married, it was just the two of us, yet we were working together towards something bigger – a home and a family. When we finally had children, my life was mapped out in raising them. Even when they grew up I was enthusiastic about my role as their mother. I wanted to hear how school was, or how their date went, or how their friends were. Now that excitement and enthusiasm has been replaced by more than just boredom, but loneliness and emptiness. There is a real void that can't be filled. That part of our lives is over and will never be again. It's back to just Tom and I but with no specific future in mind.

Now we have to rebuild our lives with just the two of us as husband and wife, and that's not simply a matter of redirecting goals, it's reforming and reshaping goals from the ground up. We need to start looking forward to things again, finding interests for ourselves as a couple and filling the gaps left by the loss of the kids, even though we know those gaps will never totally be filled. Right now, we are still on shaky ground with no definite direction or plan. It takes energy and courage to rebuild, and we're still mustering both, but we know we have to work at it. The alternative is to be cemented in boredom.

There are times when I am unhappy and discontent, but I think only half of that is related to the loss of the kids. I have never been content with myself as a person, and that low self-esteem tries to swallow me every so often until I can start thinking in a more positive frame of mind. In some ways I am stronger than I used to be and feel much more confident about myself, other days those old fears creep in and I get so low you can scoop me off the floor. I think it's part of my sensitivity and my way of handling things. When someone steps on my toes, I draw back. I nicknamed that my "puppy-dog syndrome." You can kick me and kick me, but if you come back and say, "Oh, Janet, how are you?" I lap it up, like a puppy. I'm hurt, but I'm willing to forgive and forget a lot. I think it's my overall low self-esteem that throws me into those highs and lows. It's not other people, it's just my own self.

I do feel I can tolerate more now than I used to, though. I feel stronger, tougher, more calloused since I've had to deal with the loss of the kids. Actually, some of my fears started to dissipate after Diane's husband, Larry, died. In fact, I always tell people I grew up when I was forty. After losing Larry, even though it hurt terribly, I wasn't nearly as afraid of things as I used to be. I suppose I finally realized what could happen to people – their lives cut short. I learned there was more to life than being afraid. I couldn't keep myself in that small cell anymore; I felt my fears weren't worth ruining or hanging up my life. Then to watch Diane and her kids – why should I be afraid when they obviously had the courage to go on?

I hit rock bottom after I lost the kids. What fears I had left after Larry have all but evaporated now. How much more can I hurt? Where can I go? Except to lose Tom or other close family there's nothing left for me to be afraid of. With that comes a sense of freedom. I don't carry around the heavy burden of needless worries or plaguing fears. It's like I am finally breathing with a full chest of air. Amazing, isn't it, how such tragedy could result in greater self-freedom? It's almost sad to think that. I've lost something, but I've gained something else, even though that gain is certainly not equal. You can't live everyday in fear. That's not living.

It's amazing the way people learn things. Even in pain, we can still grow. It sounds like a cliché, but it's true. For every bad thing something good will come out of it. Well, in losing your children, you can't get anywhere near believing that totally, but even I learned to be more of a free spirit.

I haven't resolved yet how to deal with these highs and lows in my life. When people say something that hurts me, I'm not assertive enough to tell them how I feel. I'm always in the "recoil" mode. Even though my moods still fluctuate, though, the lows don't seem to occur as frequently or last as long. I am able to see the triviality and pettiness in people's complaints and moaning. Sometimes I just want to tell people to get a life! Things could be worse!

The way I feel about myself and what I've accomplished in my life is still as low as it ever was, however. This is something that wasn't altered by the loss of my children. In this rebuilding phase that Tom and I are going through, I often wonder what I can do to build my own self-esteem. Sometimes I think I'm getting less interested in my self-esteem. At my age, what am I going to do? I don't feel like I should invest much time and energy in myself because it's not worth it. That's the Janet from years ago talking, not the Janet that needs to fill the void and emptiness. Lifting up my self-esteem would probably do quite a bit to fill those voids. I think I just have to learn to be happy with who I am, and maybe that's not so bad. I don't want to be the focus of attention. I like that saying, "Don't walk in front of me, don't walk behind me, just walk beside me and be my friend." That's my ideal, for people to be supportive and caring and compassionate and let me be that way in return.

I always enjoyed people and always liked to watch them in their day-to-day activities. I rarely got up to dance because I thought I would embarrass myself, yet I enjoyed observing others. I was never one of those people who really enjoyed life and let it all hang out, but since Larry and the loss of Jill and Jeff I find myself observing people even more. I don't criticize them or find fault with them, I just look at them and wonder what their lives are like. Do they have joy or sadness? Or I will look at teenagers and wonder if they'll be blessed with a long life and achieve the things they're working towards. I just look at people in a different way and hope the best for them.

I suppose I am more aware of what can happen in life. My mother-in-law will sometimes say, "I'm old, and when you're old you just never know what's going to happen." But I remind her that she's lost one son and two grandchildren at a young age, so why would she say that since she's old, she could die tomorrow? Yes, people get old and they die, but young people die too, and that's a cold fact I live with every day. We all might die at any time. People can be labeled "terminally ill" but are still alive today, whereas people who were healthy the day before aren't.

Death opens your eyes to a lot of things. It makes you think and listen a bit more. It enables you to hear what people are really saying and reset your priorities.

Where do I belong? Tom and I have to work to find our new niche. In the meantime, we keep participating in everyday life. I talk to my brother and sister every day. We are blessed with a great family. I am still close to Diane, who got remarried, by the way, to my second cousin no less! I wasn't the one who introduced them, but when I found out who she was dating I was sure surprised! The four of us go out to dinner together every Friday night.

Now that our friends and family are all "empty nesters," that has helped. It seems we are all in an equal position, of sorts. Their kids are away and so are ours. They are redefining their lives and so are we.

With Tom around the house more, he has started helping with the cleaning and even some cooking. I've learned he doesn't like to dust! He'll help with the vacuuming and other chores, however, especially with me making suggestions here and there. I will say, "Well, here's some things you could do today, and if you want to that's fine. If not, that's okay too." Over time he's picked up more and more because he's been home more and seen me do them. At work, there's another woman whose husband retired, and we were laughing about how if the food doesn't jump out of the refrigerator at them, they won't know what to eat. If I suggest, "Let's have hamburgers for dinner tonight," Tom might call me at work and say, "There isn't any meat in the refrigerator." Where does he think food comes from if you don't go to the grocery store? So he is in for a whole new education, and I'm the teacher.

I hope at some point Tom can develop a little initiative. Although he's a hard worker, he's never been a planner. He will say, "Let's go somewhere, let's do something."

I'll say, "Fine, what do you want to do?"

"Well, I don't know," is the standard reply. I told him maybe once a month we should take a weekend and get away, but then where do we go? "Where do *you* want to go?" We both get bummed out. I'm tired of making all the plans and being the ringleader.

When weddings or baby showers come up, we do our best to participate. When it's an event that we'll never experience with our children, the feelings of sorrow come flooding back to us. Those events are still a part of life and we can't stop living, and that bit of self-encouragement keeps replaying in my mind. There may be a few tears, but I usually make it through the event or at least until the trip home. I want those children's lives to be happy and to go on, just as I wish Jill's and Jeff's would have. I want to be there celebrating with them. I think the most difficult function we attended was the wedding of Jeff's girlfriend from high school. Although they broke up a couple of years before his death, her wedding caught me very emotionally. I made it through dinner, and then she came over to Tom and me and said a few things about

Jeff. I didn't want to ruin her wedding so I just wished her well and excused myself. We left shortly afterwards. Life goes on. You can't deny someone the happiness you so desperately wanted for your own kids, although you can't hide from the hurt either.

A multitude of events occur that trigger acute memories of our loss, and we're going to have to live with that the rest of our lives. Over time we've both learned to deal with it in a little better way, but it's still a constant reopening of a wound and a sharp reminder of all the dreams that will never be realized. Just recently, for example, there was a very serious accident nearby and a twenty-one-year-old girl was killed, and that brought it all back. Every time I pick up a newspaper and see a tragedy involving a young person, I relive the agony of emotion and feel such deep sorrow for the family. Almost immediately the tears well up in my eyes, but I try my best not to cry outwardly in front of other people. My grief is something I have to carry, and I don't want it spilling over on others. I cry in the car on my way home from work, or in the shower, or at night in bed. That's how I deal with the opening of the wounds. I cry when I'm alone.

Something unique happened to me recently. There is a lady who works next door in our office and her daughter and Jill knew each other. When her daughter had her baby she always brought her for me to see, as though she wanted to share her with me. One day this lady's mother passed away and she walked into my office and said, "Now, I don't want you to come to the funeral. I feel like you've had enough, and I don't want you to have to be there." I never had anyone say that to me. As much as I wanted to go, I felt I would respect her wishes. People feel like we've gone through all of this and they don't expect us to come, but everyone has feelings and when you lose someone that you've loved, whether they're old or young, it will always be hurtful. I haven't ever felt that I should not go pay my respects just because of my own loss.

I want to reach out to people, but then again I wonder if I would get myself into a predicament that I couldn't handle. What's it going to do to me – again? But I would like to think I could be there for someone if they needed me. Like with that twenty-one-year-old girl who was killed. My first instinct is to write those parents a letter. I could put my name and telephone number on it, and if they felt they needed someone, they could call. I would sit and talk to them or cry with them – whatever it took or whatever they needed, and if they never called again, that would be fine. So many people have never gone through something like that. I suppose it's like anything else. You can say to someone, "Yes, kidney stones really hurt," but the feeling of hurt can't be truly understood until you have experienced it. Besides, I think reaching out to others in these situations is what Jill would have done if she had the opportunity. Could I handle it though? I just don't know. Maybe I just need more time.

# 50

# Tom

Today I live an everyday life. I get up, go to work, come home, watch TV, and go to bed. There's not much to it. We've always been homebodies, but lately we've really been in a rut. I'm bored, I think we both are. I don't know why we haven't done something about it. We're set in our ways and don't take vacations, although we used to when the kids were here. It's not that we don't enjoy traveling or that Janet's afraid to go, but for some reason we just don't. We talk about it, but that's as far as it goes. Perhaps we are going through a mild depression.

I think we really need to do something. A person always needs some time to get away from the usual hum-drum - get away and actually relax and have fun. It won't happen if we just keep talking about it. How about adding a little spice? That would be nice. I have found that since Jill and Jeff have died, no matter what we do or where we go, we still come back to the same thoughts and the same habits. Nevertheless, you need that break to recuperate – build up your batteries so you can sustain yourself and keep going.

I feel the need for change more and more. I get irritated when little things happen – things that would never have bothered me before. I noticed it especially since Jeff's death. I used to be really easy-going and it took quite a bit to get me ruffled, but not anymore. It's almost like my nerves have shut down. Sometimes I'll get aggravated at a person driving down the street - maybe he's driving too slow or forgot his turn signal, or I'll get annoyed with Janet about something. My patience is at point zero.

I cry more too than ever before. I used to be able to watch an emotional movie and not cry, but I can't do that anymore. My emotions are raw and they are constantly at the forefront. Even though I can laugh and have a good time, the pain is always there. It's like the clown who's laughing on the outside and crying on the inside. I know how he feels. Even my memory has suffered. The emotions have drained me.

There is always some discontent and unhappiness in life because of the little things that have happened, and Janet and I are no exception. My feelings of discontent, though, have been magnified by the loss of Jill and Jeff. I'm always thinking about them and the events surrounding their deaths. I feel so unsettled by it all and certainly that contributes to the discord I feel. There are so many unresolved issues, and they eat at me. I never forget about it. It wears me down. So there's the normal discontent of everyday life, plus the never-ending cloud of our loss, plus the fact that there was no resolution with Jeff's death – everything together is rotting my insides. Dying so young isn't normal. I didn't expect that and I don't understand it.

I feel for Janet because I'm getting harder to live with. I'm grouchy. Maybe it's just a phase I'm going through. There are so many things I want to do and we're not doing them, and my grouchiness might be those frustrations poking through, but I have to work through them. Either that or we need to start branching out in our routine. You can't have stress all the time; it's got to be released in some form or another.

Considering everything that's happened, it takes an abundance of energy for Janet and me to remain a cohesive unit. I find that each of us needs our own space. You have to allow space for others in your heart, but you need to reserve a spot for yourself, too. Other people can help, but there are those things you have to work through yourself. You can't expect other people to pull you through all the time.

Janet likes to say she lost some of her fears when Larry died, and when we lost the kids she shed the rest of them. Well, she's lost quite a bit, but not all of them. But I've been training her so if it's my turn to leave next, she'll be prepared. My job has always been to take care of her. We've worked through everything else, and we'll work through this as well. What could be worse than what we've already been through? Nothing could match that. Besides, she's stronger than she thinks she is. She doesn't have a lot of faith in herself or her own abilities, and I could probably help build her self-confidence much more than I do. She is more resilient than she used to be, though. She's grown; I'm sure we both have after everything that's happened.

I don't think there will ever come a time when I am not grieving the loss of Jeff and Jill. Perhaps my grief is not as constant as in the beginning, but they are always in my thoughts. Something small will happen that will trigger the memories. I have learned to live with that. I guess that's what you could call my "adjustment" to our loss; I have put it in its place and need to go on with my own life. I had to in order to survive, but I realize some people may not be able to do that. If you can't make a place for it you're going to be overwhelmed, and you won't have control over your own life. There's nothing you can do about what's happened. The only thing you can control is what's going on right now with yourself. If you want to live your life through, then you have to go on.

How do you put grief in its place? Everyone has their own way of doing it. Janet and I handle it by talking it through. If we have problems, we help each other. Push ourselves. Sometimes we don't feel like participating in things, like if the family has a get-together and we know all their kids will be there. It's difficult for us to endure those situations sometimes. Well, we've got to do it, and we help each other be strong. To sit home away from everything and everybody is not living.

I have always been concerned for my parents as well in dealing with the loss of Jill and Jeff. Before their deaths they never talked much about losing my brother Butch, who if you'll remember also died in a car accident when he was twenty-one. To this day they still get silent when Janet and I talk about Jeff and Jill. It probably stirs up emotions from long ago. They do talk more about Butch now, though, than they did before we lost our kids. I know the pain still affects them, but like us there's nothing they can do about it. They handle it, just like we handle it, and everyone does that differently.

At times I have an interest in doing things and other times I just don't. My brother Jerry and I play in a golf league on Monday nights, and I enjoy that. I even won a trophy last year, though I'm far from being Tiger Rosko. This year I had planned on working till noon and then playing golf all afternoon, but did I do that? No, I worked till 2:00 PM and then came home.

We do our best to keep our kids' memories alive. On Valentines Day we put a memorial in the paper for them, since they both died in February. Jeff's friends from his fraternity have kept in contact with us and we went to all of their weddings. Janet and I talked about that – we didn't know if we could handle it, but we decided it was appropriate to represent Jeff and show our appreciation as well. We just felt it was the right thing to do. The boys were very receptive to us being there, too, so we felt good about our decision.

I always hope that when I meet someone they won't ask me about my kids, because then I have to tell them. I explain that I have two children, but they're both deceased, and I tell them how and when they died. I feel since they asked the question and are truly interested, they should know. A friend I have at work, for instance, asked me one day about my kids, so I told him. Well that ruined that day. The next day, I asked him if he went home and hugged his kids. He said he did.

# 51

# Janet

It's difficult for me to grasp that I have had four pregnancies and I still don't have any children. They were taken from me before they were born and then they were taken from me afterwards. It makes me wonder. I don't know where I fit. There are so many children in the world desperate for some love. How could something like this happen?

Yes, I am angry with God. Where was He? Why did He let this happen? Why did He take two healthy young people who could probably have helped turn this earth around and make it a better place? Why take people who are an asset and leave others who aren't? That's the great question in my mind – the one I have no answer for. Is that where faith comes in? That's where my faith is shaken. There's no justification.

When I talk to people who are strong spiritually, they will comment, "Thank God for that" or "Thank God for this." When something terrible happens, is He not responsible for that too? How could He be responsible for all the good yet not the bad? All our lives we are taught to accept responsibility for our actions. We are not always good and not always bad, but we are responsible. Some tell me that God has given us the right to choose our paths in life, but I am quite sure many would not have chosen the path they're on.

I don't think I'll ever have an answer to these plaguing questions while I'm on this earth. One of my co-workers who lost her husband and then lost her daughter six months later told me that I am still too deep in grief to allow understanding. She tries to reassure me that one day I will wake up or realize when I least expect it the reasons for our loss. She thinks profoundly in her faith whereas my faith has always been more childlike and simple.

"Jesus loves me." I call it my "kindergarten mentality." Confusion comes for me in digging too deeply, but perhaps a greater understanding will come in time and I will just have to be patient to see things more clearly.

I can feel my anger mellowing with time. I still believe in God, and I still say my prayers every night. On those nights where my anger is a little more surfaced I'll just start talking to the kids instead, or I'll talk to all three of them. I find myself relying more on my own strength, and sometimes I still feel like God has deserted me. Like recently, I went into the hospital twice in a row with kidney stones. I said to my sister on my second admission, "You know, I prayed that everything would be okay and here I am again. He left my prayers unanswered again." On the other hand, He may have worked in a way that told the doctors, "Follow through." Even though the x-rays showed no more stones, the doctors kept checking and they did find more, and my kidneys could have been severely damaged if they hadn't. So perhaps He really was watching over me. The answer may be there, but it's so very hard to comprehend.

I would never turn away totally from my faith. It is a part of me, and I can't sift it out. Although I plan on eventually going back to church on a regular basis, it's still a struggle right now. I want to be a part of that community but with these pressing questions I don't want to feel hypocritical either. Eventually I will go back because I feel that's where I should be, and I realize too that I am blessed in many ways with my friends and family. Perhaps I am judging God too severely, or perhaps I am just not ready.

I feel that Jeff and Jill are still with me. Even though I have unsettled feelings spiritually, I still need to believe that they are near and I will see them again. I talk to them out loud. I want them to be a part of us. I mention them in conversations just like they were still here. It makes me feel whole because it draws them back into my life, my reality.

Over time my level of grief has diminished, and I can now on occasion take a deep breath from sorrow. I don't believe I miss them any less, but I handle it better on a day-to-day basis. Even though I still carry the anguish with me I can put it on the shelf and say, "I can't think about this right now." Sometimes something very trivial can push it off the shelf and back into my lap, like a song or a picture or a familiar face. Then I caution myself, "Okay, Janet, now you have to dry those tears and get the red out of your face because you're almost at work, and you just can't have this." I talk to myself like that all the time, "Hey, cool it. Get a hold of yourself."

    I try to keep my grief to my private time. I don't want anyone else feeling uncomfortable; it's my grief and I have to live with it. It's not anyone else's fault and it's not their problem. I only talk about the kids in a happy way or reflect upon memories that were good. When I'm with someone, I can only talk about them so long and then I have to laugh or change the subject, and there are still days when I can't talk about them at all. When I do mention them, I notice that people tighten up a bit. They probably feel uncomfortable because they don't want to imagine themselves in the same position or because they care and feel badly.

    I expect that as more time passes I'll be able to handle my grief even better. I realize I have cried enough tears to fill an ocean. Even if the tears are falling, though, I don't want the people around me to worry. I'll be okay. Please, just follow through with whatever you're doing. I'll be alright.

    I feel no fear for my own death anymore. When I was younger and had Jeff and Jill to raise, I worried about dying, but now there's nothing to worry about. I can't control it and the kids are on the other side waiting anyway. There's no reason for me to be afraid. Tom and I are both sufficient enough that even though the hurt would be there if we lost each other, we know we could survive. We are both approaching the natural conclusions to our lives. If death comes tomorrow, so be it. I hear people say things like, "I don't know if we should travel, the highways are going to be busy." So what? If you stay home a car could run right through the living room. That's one thing I've learned from the loss of Jill and Jeff – you can't worry about all those things. You can't protect yourself or run and hide from death; it will find you wherever you are. Every person wants to live a long and healthy life. We don't always have that choice.

My own death even brings me a sense of peace in knowing I will be with my children again. So, in a way, I look forward to it. That doesn't mean I'm going to commit suicide tomorrow or even live recklessly, but I do long for the time we'll be together again.

Because no one knows how much time they have or what's going to happen tomorrow they should live every day to the fullest and do what is in their hearts. Everyone has limitations and everyone lives life differently, and no one way is right or wrong. We should just remember that tomorrows aren't always going to be there. Don't live a life where you look back and find many regrets. I think I have a lot of regrets.

I learned quite a bit from Jill and Jeff in their short time with me and I know others gained from them as well. I never wanted them to be quitters and neither of them was. Every hurdle that came their way, they just jumped over it. They had push, and they were able to endure.

I also learned the importance of caring for others through Jill and Jeff. They were both such kind and generous people. They were never ones to judge others for the way they looked or the clothes they wore. They weren't attracted to name brand or popular trends. They bought things because they liked them, that's all. It was the same way with people. They looked at the quality of the individual. They were not ones to put others down.

I also learned from them that many times when I didn't think they were listening, they were. They would say something perhaps a month later that let me know they were. So when you think someone's not listening, think again.

I have also grown from their deaths. I feel there is no challenge in life I wouldn't be able to handle. I have learned to focus on the positive. It amazes me how much time people spend in negativity. They waste their lives and other's too; they could spend their energy for greater good. And worrying! I worried so many years about everything. My family still accuses me of worrying to some degree, but I worry a fraction of what I did before. I have realized worrying doesn't change anything.

I have learned there is so much in life that is trivial. People complain about ridiculous things – all the garbage and excess baggage we carry. We spend so much time on the small hassles in life and neglect to see what's really important. People don't appreciate what they have. We get so wound up in our everyday routine, we lose ourselves. We never consider that tomorrow the person we love may not be there.

I wish I could impart comfort to other parents who have lost a child. I would like them to know that fortunately in time they will learn to adapt to their grief and go on. They may not want to or think they will be able to, but they will. People do go on; their lives just take a different direction. We don't always have a choice to our life's direction, but we have to keep moving and keep close to the ones we have left. Know too that even in those different paths, happiness can still be found. It's not as though the sorrow lessens or you forget about your loss, because you don't. There will be fewer tears and you'll be able to handle your grief and live your life.

Sitting and talking with people about the one you have lost, reminiscing, exploring your memories and theirs, and being aware of your own feelings will also help ease your sorrow. It allows different avenues of thinking and enables you to broaden your scope, rather than going about your lives mundanely day after day. You can't allow yourself to get stuck in a rut. Keep focusing on the horizon. Some people even suggest keeping a diary or journal, just to focus some of your attention inward. Do some soul-searching.

Talk to your surviving children as well about how they are dealing with the loss. I regret not talking to Jeff more after Jill's death. I never realized the depth of his own suffering because of it, and I never allowed him to share mine.

I would like parents to know they will have good days and bad. I would encourage them to think about the happy times and memories and be thankful they had the opportunity to have their child with them, even for a short time.

For those people wanting to help others who are dealing with a loss, I can't say to do this or that. I think you have to wait and see what that person needs – what their reactions are going to be to their loss. They may want to talk, or they may want to be isolated. Wait and see where you could fit in, where you could help or do something to alleviate their stress. Give them some space and try not to judge them or push your thoughts onto them. Make them aware that you're there for them if they want to talk or go for coffee – whatever. Talking does a lot of good. People can get into a tunnel zone where they are stuck on the loss of their loved one, and talking things through broadens their horizons.

What of my own future? I will continue to go on as best as I can without Jill and Jeff and gradually find new ways to fill my life. Working on this book has brought Tom and me even closer because he now feels more open to talk about the kids. I would like to find a place in the country or by a quiet lake where I can sit and drink my coffee, back to my roots I suppose. I want peace.

I don't have a future with my children, but I do have a future. I realize that I will always be over-emotional – I always have been, but I've cried so many tears. I want this sadness that is like an ever-present cloud over my head to be lifted. I realize too that I may be the only one who can lift it.

It's hard to sum up two very special lives. All the things they're never going to see, never going to be a part of. They worked so hard to achieve their goals. I have never felt sorry for myself, but for Jill and Jeff. They didn't get to fulfill their dreams. They weren't allowed to go on, when the best part of their life was still to come.

I will always be proud of my children – of their loving and giving ways and all they accomplished in their short time here. They touched so many people in so few years. We are blessed with their memory to hold in our hearts forever.

# 52

# Tom

The similarities between Jill's and Jeff's deaths are almost eerie. Both died on a Thursday in February. Both were twenty-one-years-old and juniors in college. Jeff was in his last session as a co-op at the General Electric plant, Jill was in her last clinical at the Michigan City hospital. Both died at the scene of the accident. The car that Jill was riding in was struck by a van, and Jeff was struck by a van. The weekends before their deaths were both particularly exciting for them. And then there are the similarities to my brother's death. He was also twenty-one-years-old. I was seventeen when he died, just like Jeff was seventeen when Jill died. He died as a result of head injuries from a crash and so did Jill and Jeff.

Are these all coincidences? Is God trying to tell us something? Is there a higher purpose in all this? Is there something we need to learn? Was it just their time? Maybe it was our fault – something we did or didn't do. These questions plague me. I am always wondering why all this had to happen, and I always carry the feeling that we were partially responsible. Was there something I could have done differently to prevent it?

I still feel God exists. He and I are just having this problem right now, you see. Even though I hold firm to my basic Catholic teachings, I can't go to church and practice my beliefs without feeling hypocritical, or maybe this "problem" as I call it is really just an excuse. It's confusing and unsettling for me. I just don't feel like I belong in church right now, because though I have tried for years I still cannot imagine why these deaths were necessary.

You can sit in church and listen to all the preaching about how God takes care of you and watches over you, but that just doesn't make sense in our case. You hear about God's miracles.

Well, why didn't He intervene when it came to my children? I don't hate God, and I'm not even angry at this point. I am not confused about God and His existence or His teachings. What I am confused about is how they apply to me. I can't listen to sermons about God being the Protective Father and then consider my own life and not see evidence of that at all.

Perhaps this is where faith comes into play. You believe even though you cannot see. I do know I want to go back to church one day. I want to participate and feel like I belong. It is my life's foundation, and I want and need that security. I want that normalcy back and I desperately need the peace and strength that normalcy imparts.

Realistically, I don't think we'll ever find that kind of peace in this life again. At the very least, getting back to the church may help us carry on with our lives and reset ourselves for the future that awaits us, and because of my ingrained beliefs I feel I need to live my life within the church in order to rejoin my family in Heaven. I have a better chance of being with my children again if I practice my religion, and perhaps there is the possibility I will find some strength and contentment.

Nobody ever pushes us to go back to church. Father Jerry, who I still play golf with, naturally says he would like us back, but he has an easy way of handling things and leaves the choice up to us. I am sure at some point we'll go back. I won't guarantee we'll stay there, but we'll try.

I do know with all my heart that Jeff and Jill are with me in spirit. I just know it, like you know there's a God. I know they're with God. How could they not be? I feel their presence in my life. When we get a thunderstorm or a snowstorm, I'll say, "Okay Jill, quit it now." Or I'll get in the car and turn on the radio and there's one of the songs from the funeral. We can relate to a lot of things that happen. Signs appear that you just know are them, if you are attentive enough to see those signs. I feel it inside and it lightens my heart to know they are communicating with me. It's not something to be afraid of – it's something to be happy about. They still have their sense of humor, too. The other day I was out driving in Jeff's Mustang. I was stopped at a light when a young man pulled up beside me in a Lexus. The light changed and we took off at the same speed, and then the guy put the pedal down and zoomed past me. At the next light we were together again. I coaxed, "Now Jeff, just settle down. We're not going to do this." The light changed, and I floored it! That car had a Purdue license plate, by the way. Anyway, I really know they're there. Other people don't notice those signs, but Janet and I do. It gives us hope.

Losing Jeff and Jill has taught me quite a bit about life. Certainly you should never take it for granted. No matter what you do or how you steer your children, that doesn't mean they're going to be safe or even happy. Life may throw you a curve – you've got to watch – you can never be prepared for what happens. When you think you are prepared, something will prove you wrong. Life knocks you off balance, and just when you think the worst has happened – it hasn't. There's always something worse.

I've learned you really don't have control of life. When times get bad, you just roll with those punches. I'm just an average person with no particular strengths or outstanding qualities. I even used to be easy-going! I'm not an expert at dealing with life, but you have to deal with it the way it is, not the way you want it to be.

Losing Jeff and Jill has also taught me about love. I love them more today than ever before because I miss them so. I appreciate them more today than ever before.

I also found compassion in people – more than I ever believed possible. People are much more caring than you would think; it's amazing how kind they can be. It's sad that it took my children's deaths to help me realize that. People are at their best when times are the worst.

I am so proud of the way Jeff and Jill lived their lives. They both knew what they wanted and devoted themselves to reaching their goals. Even though the work was hard, that's what they wanted, and that's what they did. That's something I always faulted myself for. I set very few goals at their age and didn't live up to the ones I set. I admired them so much for their self-discipline.

In living with my own grief these years, I've found that people who hide everything and don't talk about their grief are the ones you have to worry about the most. It's not healthy to shut it all in. Bring it out into the open. The more you talk about it - and it is hard to talk about sometimes - the better off you are. Believe too that the ones you've lost are there to hear.

I would encourage family and friends to ask questions and also share their sorrow. If you are sitting with a person you know is hurting but you don't talk about what's bothering them or are afraid to broach the subject because you don't want to cause them further distress, what good have you accomplished? Perhaps that person is waiting for you to say something, wanting to talk about it, but they don't bring it up because they don't want to burden you. It's important to keep the memories alive and that's how you keep them alive. That's how you keep them with you. If you never talk about them, they are dead. Keep them in your heart and in your mind. Talk about them and talk *to* them. Then they're not really dead, they're just in another place.

In talking to other people, you also gleam different perspectives on your loss. It opens your eyes to some new ideas and gives you fresh avenues to explore. Working your mind like that helps relieve some of the pressures of your grieving and expands your knowledge on how life works. It can offer new hope and further your courage to face another day.

It's not an easy thing to lose a child, and I don't know if it ever gets better. You learn to deal with it more constructively as time goes by. You have good times and bad, times when you laugh and others when you cry. You'll deal with it differently than someone else may, but you have to find what works for you. What else can you do? Become a hermit perhaps and close everything inside. You might as well bury yourself if you stay that deep in your grief.

With my own grief, I can't predict from day to day how I'll feel. I may go three or four days thinking about the kids and everything's fine. Then I might have that one day where sorrow pulls me down. Maybe something specific triggers it and maybe not. I just take every day as it comes and not wonder about tomorrow. I live for today because I already know I can't control what tomorrow brings. That's the most profound lesson I've learned. You can plan tomorrow and your future and work towards it, but that doesn't necessarily mean it's going to happen. You can hope tomorrow brings what you've planned, but if it doesn't, you'll just have to deal with it.

Sometimes I say that Janet and I don't have a future, but that's not really true. We do have a future, but it's a lonely future. It's just the two of us, and yes that's something, but it's not the future we planned. All of a sudden at our age we have to shift gears, and it's hard to do that. We've worked all our lives towards specific goals with our family, and now those goals aren't there anymore. What can we do? The choice before us now is to redirect our energies or stay in our rut. We have to refocus our direction, but it takes a long, long time. We're getting through it slowly, and it's a process that will take years. We started the shift when Jill died and then again after Jeff. We started our new future then, even though we didn't think of it that way at the time. Every day we live, we are living for the future until God decides to move us to a better place.

Jill and Jeff were just normal kids. They were hard-working and full of fun. They were on the verge of realizing their dreams. We learned a lot about them after they died, like how friendly they were, the kindness they showed other people – stories we had no idea about because they wouldn't come home and tell us those things. I wish I could find the words that adequately impart how much we loved our children and how special they were, how much they meant to our lives and the lives of others. There are no words to express the depth of our sorrow, no words to communicate the endless void in our hearts.

# *Author's Note*

    *I was one of the many fortunate people who actually knew Jill and Jeff, however casually. I was Diane's neighbor, and I visited with Tom and Janet sporadically over the course of several years as Jill and Jeff grew to young adulthood. I vividly remember Jill's lilting laugh and her enthusiasm for just about everything life had to offer, and I remember Jeff's quiet, shy mannerisms and sparkling eyes that belied the mischief within. I recall Janet and Tom when they were totally absorbed with the everyday concerns of parents with growing children, trying to keep up as best as they could. Each of us that knew the four of them, however slightly, has their unique recollections.*

    *My own daughter was a nursing student at Valparaiso University the same time Jill and the other girls were killed, and news of their deaths did in fact shake the community. My family attended the wake, and I remember how difficult it was to even walk through the doors of the funeral home, understanding with a full finality that it could easily have been my own daughter. Years later, when my husband phoned me from work one day telling me the news of Jeff's loss, a disbelief that such a tragedy could strike again ran through me like shock waves. Through it all, Tom and Janet maintained themselves with quiet dignity and restraint, while the rest of us who looked on wondered how we would have managed to maintain simple sanity.*

    *When I approached Tom and Janet in January of 2001 with the idea of writing this book, I wasn't at all sure what their reaction would be. Perhaps I had not waited long enough for them to come to terms with their loss to rehash it in detail, but they immediately agreed to the project, and together we formulated four goals. Certainly we wanted the book to serve as a memorial to Jill and Jeff as well as help others deal with the process of grief. We also wanted to explore from two different viewpoints their lives* and the marks they left, and hopefully put these events into some perspective, gleaming understanding from them.

As I sat across from Tom and Janet for nearly eighteen months, prompting their individual memories, I couldn't help but wonder how I would have fared in similar circumstances. Certainly not as well. The reliving and retelling of so many memories alone took great courage, and this from two people who proclaimed themselves simple and with few accomplishments, and particularly from a woman who declared herself riddled with long-term fears of life, who in fact I found to be the strongest and most courageous woman I've ever met. They have both survived, and survived with a quiet and unobtrusive dignity and clarity of purpose I have rarely seen. They endeavor merely to go on.

They both talked frequently about the many coincidences of Jill and Jeff's deaths and even of Tom's brother's death many years before. I for one do not believe in coincidence. I believe now more than ever that there are higher purposes for what we endure in our lives. I have asked myself many times after meeting with Tom and Janet "why" these things had to happen. What possible good could come out of it? I have grown to understand, however, that the "why" is not nearly as important as what we can learn from it, as well as what we do with the knowledge we have gained. I trust the "why" will be answered at some point beyond, but today we can all learn and grow from this family's experiences.

I believe one of the great truths of this world is that we are all connected, and every life is meant to teach. I have learned from Jeff and Jill. I have learned to appreciate family and the love that is so freely offered to me. When my own grown children now ask me to watch a movie or go to dinner with them or stop and talk for a moment, I stop what I'm doing and do it, realizing that every moment is precious and wanting to share in and return their affection. I've opened my life to those I love and said the words we too often forget to say.

I have recalculated my priorities and put people and relationships first.

*I have also redefined the relationship I have with myself, knowing that is the greatest relationship I will ever have. I try to live without fear. I try to devote myself to the simple pleasures of the present rather than the hauntings of the past or the uncertainties of the future.*

*I have also learned that you can't hide from grief. It is a process much more than the five simple "stages" we read about in medical literature. It is part of our progression through life and includes defined decision-making, an affirmation to love, and self-sacrificing forgiveness. Grief becomes enmeshed in the fabric of our very souls and does not wear away over time, rather we absorb it into our redefined self.*

*Most of all, I have learned that love never dies. Tom and Janet love Jill and Jeff now as much as they ever did. As I believe that thoughts and emotions have power and substance, I also believe that the love they continually send to Jeff and Jill is received and returned threefold.*

*Tom and Janet carry their grief as a heavy burden. Throughout our many months of working together, I saw flickers of life returning to their routine. I would like to see them progress even further to regain their lives and rediscover the happiness within, yet I understand this will take constant commitment, self-motivation, and tremendous courage on their part. In mourning the relationships they had with their children, they have forgotten the relationship they have with themselves. Making a conscious decision to live their lives to the utmost is a substantial first step. They each have a great capacity to love and share their warmth with others, and daring to do that without fear of further hurt or loss is the second rung of healing. Lastly, I believe finding forgiveness in their hearts for the suffering and loss they have endured will bring them full circle and allow them the lasting peace and wholeness for which they yearn.*

*I have been honored by Tom and Janet's willingness to share their lives and memories with me, and I hope they will continue to do so in times ahead. I wish them both the peace they so richly deserve.*

# *Epilogue*

Six months after my last "official" meeting with Tom and Janet, I spent a February morning with them catching up on all that had been happening in their lives. Tom was proud to show off his newly purchased '93 Corvette and was anxious for the weather to break to get it on the road again. Together they had redecorated their dining room and living room and had already started early spring cleaning. They had taken a family vacation to visit relatives in Florida, and Janet confided that was the first vacation where she felt relaxed and not at a rush to get home. In another month they would be accompanying friends to Las Vegas, with Tom proclaiming that would be their first "real" vacation in nine years. They were also re-acclimating themselves to church, having attended several services with plans to continue.

Not a day passes that Jill and Jeff are not close in their memories, and that will never change. In the meantime they are reclaiming life, one step at a time.

## *About the Author*

    Renee' Kimberling, a native of Northwest Indiana, is a registered nurse, graduating magna cum laude from Valparaiso University. Certified in gerontology, she has held various staff and administrative positions in the long-term care arena, as well as being guest lecturer for multiple health care organizations. She enjoys teaching and has authored numerous continuing education programs for medical professionals throughout the years. In 1990, she founded Horizon Career College and served as its President for six years, and since then has consulted for program and staff development issues. She and Ron, her husband of thirty years, have two children and two grandchildren and currently reside in Wheatfield, Indiana.

Photographs Courtesy of:

Wedding Photo of Tom and Janet Rosko *Giolas Photographers, Inc. 7994 Broadway Merrillville IN. 46410*

Senior Picture of Jill and Jeff Rosko By Gary St. Martin of *St. Martin's Photography Studio 2990 W. US HWY 30 Merrillville, IN. 46410*

Family Photo showing Tom, Janet, Jill and Jeff *Olan Mills Studio, Inc. 31 W. $78^{th}$ Ave. Merrillville, IN. 46410*

Basketball Photo of Jeff Rosko *Olan Mills Studio, Inc. 31 W. $78^{th}$ Ave. Merrillville, IN. 46410*

Photo of Jill and Jeff Rosko *Olan Mills Studio, Inc. 31 W. $78^{th}$ Ave Merrillville, IN. 46410*

Printed in the United States
15744LVS00004B/257